"I'm Being Paid To Find My Client A Husband, Jake...."

"not to fall in love with you myself!"

Jake went very still. "Fall in love with?"

Dani stared at him, then flushed. "That's not what I meant."

"You said fall in love with," he reminded her, curious as to what she *had* meant.

Dani seemed flustered, and her cheeks were pink. "I know what I said," she snapped. "It was just a slip, that's all. For heaven's sake, you don't have to look at me like that—I'm not going to do something stupid like falling in love with you and...and making this all messy. I told you, I don't even believe in love."

"Yeah, so you did." For some reason, he didn't find her assurance half as satisfying as he should have. Frowning, he walked to where she was standing and put his hands on her shoulders, turning her to face him. "Your client has nothing to do with this, Buttercup. This is something between you and me."

Dear Reader:

As you can see, Silhouette Desire has a bold new cover design that we're all excited about. But while the overall look is new, two things remain the same. First, we've kept our eye-catching red border. You can be sure to always spot Silhouette Desires on the shelves! Second, between these new covers are the high-quality love stories that you've come to expect.

In addition, the MAN OF THE MONTH program continues with Mr. September, who comes from the pen of Dixie Browning. Clement Cornelius Barto is a unique hero who is sure to charm you with his unusual ways. But make no mistake, it's not just *Beginner's Luck* that makes him such a winner.

October brings you a man who's double the fun, because not only is Jody Branigan an exciting hero, he's also one of Leslie Davis Guccione's Branigan brothers. Look for his story in *Branigan's Touch*.

We at Silhouette have been happy to hear how much you've all enjoyed the Year of the Man. The responses we've received about the special covers— and to each and every one of our heroes—has been enthusiastic. Remember, there are more men ahead in 1989—don't let any of them get away!

Yours,

Lucia Macro
Senior Editor

NAOMI HORTON

THE IDEAL MAN

SILHOUETTE *Desire*

Published by Silhouette Books New York

America's Publisher of Contemporary Romance

SILHOUETTE BOOKS
300 East 42nd St., New York, N.Y. 10017

ISBN: 0-373-05518-8

First Silhouette Books printing September 1989

Printed in the U.S.A.

Books by Naomi Horton

Silhouette Romance

Risk Factor #342

Silhouette Desire

Dream Builder #162
River of Dreams #236
Split Images #269
Star Light, Star Bright #302
Lady Liberty #320
No Walls Between Us #365
Pure Chemistry #386
Crossfire #435
A Dangerous Kind of Man #487
The Ideal Man #518

NAOMI HORTON

was born in northern Alberta, where the winters are long and the libraries far apart. "When I'd run out of books," she says, "I'd simply create my own—entire worlds filled with people, adventure and romance. I guess it's not surprising that I'm still at it!" An engineering technologist, she has recently moved to Nanaimo, British Columbia, with her collection of assorted pets.

Prologue

Have You Got What It Takes? In a world filled with mediocrity, my client is looking for that one man out there with that Something Special. She's a modern-day woman who has it all: except that special man in her life to make it perfect. But she won't settle for second best. If you're a modern-day hero with those old-fashioned ideals of strength, honor and courage, if you're kind, gentle and loving, if you're independent and can support a lady in style, then maybe—just *maybe*—you have what it takes. If you think you do, send us a detailed résumé telling us why. But be prepared to prove it! My client has a lot to offer that special man—obviously we expect a lot from you. Meeting our standards isn't going to be easy, but the reward will be well worth the challenge. Send correspondence to Danielle Ross, ManHunters Incorporated.

One

―――――

What you need," Buster Greaves muttered truculently, "is a wife." He twisted the angel's left wing, trying to align it with her right one.

"What I *need*," Jake mumbled through a mouthful of straight pins, "is a miracle!"

Buster gave the angel's wing another twist that made her squeak in protest. "These danged things gonna stay on, you suppose?"

"I hope they fall off!" The small golden-haired angel between them twisted around to glower ferociously at her wings. They arched over her head, bent and soiled with fingerprints. "I don't know why I hafta wear these dumb things, anyway! Everybody's gonna laugh and that dumb Robby Jacobsen's gonna—"

"Stand still," her frazzled father growled, shoving a pin through the gauzy fabric near the hem of her dress. "Ow! Damn it, Cassie, stand still!"

The angel gave him an affronted look. "You're not supposed to swear at angels, Daddy."

"If this particular angel would stand still," Jake reminded her darkly, "she wouldn't get sworn at!"

"Well, I'm tired." Cassie stood on one leg to scratch a mosquito welt on her ankle. "I've been standing here for hours! I'm tired. And I hafta go to the bathroom."

"You went five minutes ago," Jake reminded her with an immense calm he didn't actually feel. "It won't kill you to stand still for five more minutes until I get this *blasted* hem straight!"

Cassie gave a huge, impatient sigh and scratched her ankle with her other foot. Jake glared at her, and she straightened with a flounce, muttering something decidedly unangelic under her breath. It earned her a gentle rap on the top of her head from her great-grandfather, and a sharp look of disapproval from Jake. "Where did you pick *that* up from?"

Cassie shrugged, fidgeting. "Jesse said it yesterday when the roan stepped on his foot."

"When you're Jesse's age, you can use language like that. Maybe. When you're six, forget it."

"Six and a half, nearly," Cassie reminded him sulkily. "And besides, Robby Jacobsen says worse things than that. Yesterday, when Kevin O'Donnel punched him, he said—"

"I don't want to hear it!" Jake held up a restraining hand, shaking his head in despair over his daughter's vocabulary. Raised in a houseful of earthy, hardworking men, she was a perplexing blend of angelic sweetness one moment and pugnacious tomboy the next, and the truth of it was that she could outride, outsmart and outcuss just about everybody on Silvercreek Ranch—including him. "Okay, that's the best I can do for now. Take it off and I'll turn the hem up after Jesse and I have finished repairing the corral fence."

The angel gave a Rebel yell that made the yellow hound in front of the fireplace leap to his feet. Filmy gown and golden wings went flying, and the angel, clad more normally now in jeans and T-shirt, bolted for the door.

"Hey!" Jake's bellow brought her up short. "You're not going anywhere until you finish that project for Miss Wilson."

"It's *Ms.* Wilson," Cassie said loftily, "and I finished it already."

"You managed to collect a boxful of leaves and pressed flowers," Jake reminded her calmly. "All you have to do now is glue them onto that sheet of construction paper so they can be displayed in class. Shouldn't take you more than...oh, an hour."

"Ahhh!" Cassie flounced back into the room, her expression one of pained impatience. "Cochise said he'd help me make a real Indian warbonnet outta them feathers we—"

"Those feathers," Jake corrected wearily. "And it's 'out of,' Cassie. Two words. Cochise is out dredging a pond for the ducks. He can help you with the warbonnet tonight after supper."

"But I gotta go to that dumb play rehearsal tonight," she protested, her small dirty face screwing up with distress.

"Cassie, give me a break." Her father started gathering up glitter dust and stray pins, sparing her a tolerant look. "You were the one who was whooping and hollering a couple of months ago about being in this play—so quit making it sound like capital punishment. And you've got an entire summer ahead of you to make as many warbonnets as you want. Trust me."

Cassie stared at him for a moment as though judging how far he could be pushed, then capitulated with another huge sigh and turned away, shoulders drooping, feet dragging. "Don't know why I gotta glue some dumb leaves on some dumb construction paper," she muttered as she made her way toward her room. "Robby Jacobsen says his dad doesn't make *him* do that stuff. Robby Jacobsen says..."

The rest was an unintelligible mumble as she disappeared into the back of the house.

"What's with Robby Jacobsen all of a sudden?" Jake looked at his grandfather curiously, sucking his finger where he'd jabbed it with the pin. "He's all she ever talks about these days."

Buster gave a rumbling laugh. "Don't you recognize a bad case of puppy love when you see it?"

"Love?" Jake gave a snort. "She's six years old! The way she talks you'd think he was the lowest form of life on the planet."

"Don't you remember *your* first heartthrob?" Buster grinned. "Pretty little thing, as I recall. Red hair. Temper like a firecracker. Gave you one hell of a shiner back in second grade when you put that poor old frog in her locker."

Jake had to smile. "Margaret O'Donnel. And that poor old frog made out better than I did. She named him Francis and put him in a terrarium—got an A on her science project. All I got was a D minus for that display on bats I put together."

"Only because one of 'em got out and scared the living daylights out of Mrs. Sykes," Buster reminded him with a chuckle. "You never did have much luck with women."

He said it laughingly, not meaning anything by the words, yet they hit Jake like a fist in the solar plexus. He managed a rough laugh, nodded and said, turning away, "yeah."

As always he was surprised at how the old hurts could still catch him off guard. He could go for weeks without giving any of it a single thought, and then something would trigger it unexpectedly: a careless word, a peal of woman's laughter, a hint of honeysuckle on the wind. The pain, the anger, would jolt through him like an electric shock, leaving him shaken and moody for hours.

"Hey, Jake..." His grandfather's voice was suddenly soft. "Boy, I didn't mean anything by that. You know—"

"Hey, yourself," Jake retorted teasingly, forcing himself to laugh, to turn around with a careless grin he knew didn't fool the old man for a minute. But they all had their roles to play. "You sure you'll be okay at Cassie's rehearsal tonight?"

"I'll be okay," Buster grumbled, obviously relieved to be on safe ground again. "But you should be the one going with her. Jesse and me can get that corral fixed."

"Buster, we've been through this already." There was no need to add the rest: that he hadn't missed how Buster's hip had been bothering him, that stubbornness alone couldn't hold off the onset of age forever. "Besides," he added gently, trying to make it easier for the old man, "you've been helping Cass with her lines all month—you know her part almost as well as she does. I'd just be in the way."

"I doubt Ms. Wilson would see it that way," Buster said with a sly grin. "I think she fancies you, Jake. She sure spends a lot of time thinking up excuses to phone here."

"All we talk about is Cassie," Jake said patiently. "And when we're not talking about *her*, we're talking about you. I think if she fancies anyone in this family, it's you."

"You pulling my leg?" Buster looked at him suspiciously.

"I think if you did some serious courting, you could wind up with Ms. Wilson yourself."

Buster gave a grunt, obviously intrigued by the idea. "You think she'd be interested in an old coot like me?"

"Don't know why not. As far as old coots go, you're no worse than most. Even halfway decent-looking, when you bother to shave and change your shirt."

Buster rubbed the graying bristles on his chin noisily, looking down at the soiled shirt covering his ample stomach. "Meant to get some laundry done, but with that danged machine busted for the past two weeks..." He looked around the large clutter-filled living room. "Should get some of this cleaned up, too, before that ManHunter lady gets here. Wouldn't want her to get the wrong idea about us right off."

Jake, halfway to the kitchen door, stopped dead. "*What* did you just say?"

Buster, to his credit, looked suitably embarrassed. "Well, umm, I meant to tell you she was coming up to talk to you. Today, maybe. But, umm..."

Jake's whispered oath hissed through the room. Hands on hips, he glared at Buster. "I thought I told you to tell her it was all a mistake. I thought I said—"

"I know what you said," he muttered, avoiding Jake's eyes. "But, hell, boy—we need help around here. If this bum hip of mine gets much worse, I'm not going to be any use to you at all. And just trying to keep Cassie in line is a full-time job. She figures dresses are for sissies, and can fight and cuss better than most boys twice her age. That ain't no way for a little girl to grow up. She needs a woman around, Jake. A full-time woman to... to teach her things. Tell her things." Buster's weathered cheeks turned pink. "She was asking me questions about... well, about... woman things last week. A man oughtn't to be talking to a little girl about things like that!"

Buster's embarrassment was so acute that Jake nearly smiled. "I know, but damn it, you can't just order me a wife through the mail like you'd order a new harness. You don't know anything about her. You—"

"I know she wants a husband—a good husband. And I know you'd make a good one, given half a chance. I know you need a woman in your life again. The right kind of woman this time. I know Cassie needs a mother real bad."

Jake swore with impatience. "And how do you know I'm even close to what she's looking for? I'm a rancher. I know horses and I know cattle, but I've proved I don't know the first thing about women," he said.

"You must be part of what she's looking for, or she wouldn't have come all the way out here to look us over. Fact you got this far, after all them questionnaires we filled out—"

"*You* filled out. I didn't even know what was going on until a couple of months ago, remember?"

"Well, I didn't think it would do no harm," Buster grumbled.

"Any harm," Jake corrected automatically. He caught Buster's sharp look and shrugged an apology, torn as usual between annoyance at Buster's interference and guilt at that annoyance. His grandfather had only done it out of love and concern, but there were times when that concern came mighty close to being outright meddling. "The washing machine's fixed," he said with finality. "I tossed in a pile of Cassie's things—make sure she's wearing something clean before rehearsal tonight. If she turns up looking as though she hasn't seen soap and water for a week, that woman from social services will get wind of it, sure as hell." Jake gave Buster a pointed look. "And you remember what happened last time she was here."

"Said we weren't providin' a proper environment for a little girl," Buster growled indignantly.

"If she finds out that last housekeeper quit, she'll be out here like a hound on deer scent. She's not going to be happy until she gets Cassie into a foster home, dressed in pinafores and behaving like a real little lady."

"Our Cassie?" Buster gave a snort.

Even Jake had to smile at the image.

"If you had a wife," his grandfather said with a sly sidelong glance, "the problem would sort of solve itself."

"You," Jake said between clenched teeth, "are walking on thin ice. Now I'm going out there to fix that corral fence, and if this female headhunter turns up, she's *your* problem, got that? You just tell her Jake Montana isn't looking for a wife!"

As he strode into the big country kitchen, Jake wondered if he was being entirely honest with that last statement. The truth was that he had found himself wondering lately if maybe Buster wasn't onto something. Maybe an arranged marriage was the only practical kind. Two levelheaded and realistic people getting married for all the *right* reasons, whatever they happened to be, wasn't as ridiculous as it first sounded. Hell, men and women got married all the time for all the wrong reasons: love, mainly. And look what it got them.

He strode across the kitchen and out the back door. Personally it had gotten him nothing more than three years of hell. People were still talking about how he hadn't been man enough to keep his woman in his own bed, about how she'd warmed enough mattresses up and down the Cariboo to qualify for some kind of record. He caught the way they looked at him when they thought he wouldn't notice, the way they looked at Cassie, trying to see whom she resembled most—the man who was supposed to be her father, or any of the other half dozen or so who could have been.

Sandra had married him thinking he was her ticket out of the pulp and paper town she'd grown up in, and all too quickly discovered that life on a working cattle ranch wasn't much better. Bored and resentful, she'd turned to liquor, which had filled her empty days with false joy, and then to men. And she'd laughed while she'd done it. That was the worst part. She'd done it to hurt him, and had laughed when she realized how well she'd succeeded.

She'd walked out of his life nearly six years ago, abandoning the infant daughter she'd never wanted. He had no idea where she'd gone, where she was now, and he couldn't honestly say he even gave a damn. But sometimes—God, sometimes the pain was almost more than he could bear.

"Daddy!" Cassie's urgent shout, coming from the kitchen door, brought Jake's head up sharply. "The washin' machine's busted again and there's water all over!"

"I don't need a wife," he muttered as he headed back to the house at a run. "I need a maintenance engineer!"

It was, Dani Ross decided, the quintessentially perfect male backside.

It was splendidly displayed, thrust upward at a rakish angle and snugly encased in a pair of jeans. Very old jeans, Dani noticed. And very tight. They molded themselves around every inch of him as closely as an old lover and she gazed appreciatively at the play of muscle in the tight buttocks, at the way the soft, worn denim hugged every taut contour with tantalizing precision.

The man was leaning precariously over a washing machine that had recently regurgitated its wash cycle, and he was swearing gently and creatively at whatever he was working on, oblivious to her. Not in any particular hurry to break his concentration—or her own, for that matter—Dani simply leaned against the doorframe and waited. She let her gaze travel leisurely downward, taking in a truly remarkable length of denim-clad leg. The legs ended in worn, dusty cowboy boots, and Dani smiled, knowing she had found her man.

Her *Ideal Man*.

Dani smiled to herself. Maybe better than most, she knew perfectly well the Ideal Man didn't exist. After all, she'd married one herself. And still had the divorce papers to prove the lie. But when Marion Wainwright-Syms had hired her to find a husband for her sister, Dani had prudently decided to keep her opinions to herself. Marion preferred it that way. And Marion Wainwright-Syms generally got whatever she wanted.

Not that finding suitable husbands for lovelorn women was part of her job description at ManHunters Incorporated. She was a corporate recruiter—one of the best—and when Marion had come to her with this preposterous scheme, she'd laughed aloud. "My sister is going to be thirty in a few months," Marion had told Dani briskly, "and frankly, it's time she was married. Since Caroline doesn't seem able to get things moving in that direction herself, I've decided to take over. After all, I've been looking after her for most of her life. I suppose it's only natural that *this* has fallen onto my shoulders as well."

And then onto mine, Dani mused, still admiring the attributes of the man in front of her. If the rest of him came even close to the promise held in those tight jeans, it was just possible she'd found what she was looking for.

The advertisement had been the first step. Six weeks after it had appeared in all the major glossy trade and business magazines in the country, she'd been knee-deep in replies. Some had been typed on Fortune 500 letterhead, others laboriously handwritten on lined pages torn out of drugstore notebooks. Some contained photographs. Some were little more than tediously precise lists of what the correspondent wanted in a wife. Others included photocopies of bank statements and stock portfolios. Some begged, others pleaded, and there were even a few obscene ones, notable only for their lack of originality.

She'd spent weeks screening the letters. After she'd made her first culls, she'd sent lengthy and intimately detailed questionnaires to all the remaining men. There were more weeks of letters, more culls, more questionnaires. Slowly her list of candidates shrank as she weeded out the nut cases, and the hopeful but hopeless.

Three weeks ago she'd started the in-person interviews. She'd traveled from Cape Breton Island to Vancouver, and so far had narrowed the field to two, one a serious young accountant from Halifax, the other an up-and-coming Vancouver stockbroker.

And then, of course, there was the cowboy.

Rancher, Dani corrected, eyeing the perfectly filled jeans in front of her. He may *sound* like the hero in a Saturday matinee western, but Jake Montana was a legitimate rancher.

He also, at a shrewd glance, had the cutest butt in Canada.

Which didn't have anything to do with the matter at hand but was certainly a pleasant respite from the mountains and scrub brush she'd been staring at all morning.

Something hit the wall behind the washing machine with a thud. It was followed by a growl of earthy profanity, then a promising silence that ended in a querulous mutter regarding the washing machine's suspect parentage and, finally, the sound of a nut being tightened. There was a satisfied grunt, and a hand appeared from behind the machine and groped across the control panel.

Dani put her briefcase down and made her perilous way across the wet floor. "I can do this," she said helpfully. "What do you want pushed?"

"Jeez!" Badly startled, he erupted from behind the machine. He came up too fast, caught his right shoulder under a narrow shelf and sent it flying at the same instant the back of his head connected solidly with the overhanging cupboard. Dani winced as the air around them turned blue.

"You scared the hell out of me!" the man bellowed, rubbing the back of his head with one hand and cradling his wounded shoulder with the other. "You selling cemetery plots or something?"

"No," she said dryly. "Are you Jake Montana?"

He had the bluest eyes she'd ever seen in her life. They fastened onto hers like twin lasers, dangerously dark. "What's left of him. You're here to tell me I've just won a million dollars, right? I can buy my own tropical island and spend the rest of my life surrounded by palm trees, sandy beaches and naked women. And I won't have to waste another day and a half trying to fix this *blasted* machine!"

She'd known he was tall—listed as six feet and a couple of inches on the questionnaire—but for some reason she hadn't realized just how tall six feet and a couple of inches could *be*. She had to tip her head back just to meet his eyes, and even shod in three inches of Italian leather, she barely came up to his shoulder.

He smelled delicious, a seductive combination of healthy male sweat, horses and leather that she knew instinctively hadn't come out of a cologne bottle. It took an effort, but she managed to remember why she was there. "Uhh, no. Sorry. I—"

"Didn't think so. Hold this." He slapped the wrench into her hand and turned back to the washing machine.

Dani blinked at the wrench. "My name is—"

"Okay, give it to me." He reached back, fingers waggling.

Dani took a deep breath and her fingers tightened around the wrench. Maybe if she whacked him over the head a couple of times just to grab his attention....

"The wrench, the wrench!"

Refusing to give in to the temptation, she slapped the wrench into his hand as adroitly as a nurse handing instruments to a surgeon. "Wrench!" There was a mutter that could have been thanks. "I knew I shouldn't have taken on this job," she reminded herself. "Nobody told me I was going to have to put up with *this*!"

It had taken Marion nearly two weeks of arguing to get her to agree to do the job. In the end it had been sympathy for Caroline that had decided her. Twenty-nine and single and without a prospect on the horizon was how Marion had described her sister. But that had in no way prepared Dani for the tiny, painfully shy woman who had come to her office. She'd been wide-eyed and quiet, as awkward and self-conscious as a twelve-year-old, and it was obvious that she was not only in awe of her brisk, assured, corporate-director sister, but utterly intimidated, as well. How the same parents had spawned two daughters so unalike was a mystery of genetics, Dani supposed, but she couldn't help feeling sorry for Caroline. She'd sat in Dani's office with a sweet, serene smile, saying that she trusted Marion's intentions completely and that she would marry whoever Dani found for her.

Dani sighed. Her own sense of responsibility had done the rest. From that moment on, this search for Caroline's Ideal Man had become less a job than a personal quest. She'd made up her mind that she wasn't going to quit until she'd found the best possible husband for Caroline—even if it meant interviewing every eligible bachelor in North America.

So she couldn't really blame anyone but herself when she wound up in the wilds of central British Columbia playing plumber's assistant!

"When I tell you, turn the machine on. It's all set up, just push that green button."

Dani glared at the broad shoulders wedged between the machine and the wall. Ideal Man or not, this guy was pushing his luck. If he *was* her Ideal Man.

He'd certainly been high on her list, anyway. Right from the start she'd been struck by his sincerity. His letters, meticulously if inexpertly typed, had none of the ill-concealed desperation or bravado so many had. They were simply written: the personal information offered without apology or boastfulness, the realities of ranch life discussed honestly, the details of a failed marriage and subsequent divorce concise and to the point. The follow-up questionnaires provided enough information about his central British Columbia cattle operation to establish that he was a shrewd businessman who not only loved what he was doing, but was darned good at it, besides. His references were excellent, from his banker to old college professors, and it had taken little work to confirm that Montana was a respected member of his community.

He was also the most irritating person she'd met on this entire project!

"Okay, turn it on."

Dani eased a breath out between her teeth and stabbed the green button. The machine started to hum, then a hose coupling flew across the floor and Montana swore furiously. A jet of water shot out from under the machine and caught Dani across the ankles. She yelped and leaped back, nearly falling as one foot skated out from under her on the wet floor.

"Turn it off, turn it off!" came a sputtered bellow. "I'm drownin' back here! Turn it off!"

"I'm trying!" Dani scanned the panel desperately for some indication of how to do just that, then spun the wash cycle knob clockwise. Everything stopped and she took an unsteady breath, then looked down at her shoes. "My God! These are Italian leather! I paid a fortune for them and they're ruined!"

"You from social services?" Montana eased himself from behind the washing machine and tossed the wrench down with a bang. He was soaked to the shoulders and gave her a dark look as he wiped his forearm across his dripping face.

"No, I'm not from social services!" Dani slipped her feet out of nearly two hundred dollars' worth of sopping leather.

Montana grunted. "That's one thing in your favor, anyway. Seems like everytime something goes wrong around here, I'm falling over one of them. I don't suppose you saw where that coupling went, did you?"

Not having the faintest idea of how social services got into the conversation, Dani stooped down and retrieved the errant loop of metal. She dropped it into his palm.

He gave a snort of amusement and started wedging himself between the washer and its companion dryer again. He handed her the wrench, grinning cheerfully at her, then disappeared down behind the washing machine. "You're not so bad at this, after all. What did you say your name was?"

Dani took a calming breath. "Danielle Ross. I called you yesterday from Vancouver and told you I'd be here."

"Try it again."

Dani wrenched the dial to its wash cycle. Water started shooting into the tub and after it had risen two or three inches, she cycled the machine ahead so the pump came on. "Is it holding?"

"Seems to be," came the muffled reply. "No, it's leaking. No, wait a minute—it's just water from the last time." The silence grew, filled only with the hum of the machine. A thoughtful grunt emanated from behind the machine.

"Maybe I finally outwitted the little sucker. Let's wait a minute or two to make sure."

Dani sighed and found her gaze drifting down the smooth, sweep of his back. His shirt was pulled tight across his shoulders and she watched the ripple of muscle under the blue and white checks with absentminded admiration, noting the ribbon of tanned skin where his shirt had pulled out.

Is he the one? she thought idly. It was that possibility—that the *next* man she interviewed might be the right man, the Ideal Man—that had kept her going this long. It was the same kind of hope that kept gamblers playing and prospectors panning, the seductive promise that the next toss of the dice or panful of mud would be the big winner.

She sure hadn't hit any jackpot so far!

She'd started out with a fairly good idea of the kind of man she wanted. She and Caroline had talked for days about it, at times seriously making lists and writing out goal statements, at others getting giddy on too much wine and laughing, far into the night, about men and love and marriage. But in the end she was going to toss aside the lists and leave it to gut instinct. Those instincts had never failed her in six years of recruiting high-paid executives for some of the biggest, most powerful corporations in the world. She'd made her reputation on those instincts, a reputation that had made her one of the most sought-after headhunters in Canada. They wouldn't let her down now.

"You the A.I. lady?"

"A.I.?"

"Artificial insemination," he said, a trifle impatiently.

"Artificial insem—? No, I am not the—" She took a deep breath. "This is ridiculous! Will you come out from behind there so we can—"

"In a minute. I thought you were with the A.I. people." *And since you're not,* his tone said clearly, *why am I wasting time talking to you?*

"Is that thing holding?" Dani asked with forced calm.

"Yeah." He sounded pleasantly surprised. "It is." He began extricating himself from behind the machine. "You were saying . . . ?"

"I was *saying*," Dani repeated through clenched teeth, "that I'm from ManHunters Incorporated, and—"

"ManHunters?" He straightened slowly, turning to look at her. His gaze wandered over her with lazy speculation. "So. You're the one."

There was something about the way he said it, half surprise, half droll amusement, that frayed Dani's patience almost to the breaking point. That, and the way he was looking at her, his gaze running over her with a stockman's impersonal thoroughness as though estimating her worth in the auction ring.

"The one *what*?" she snapped.

Those lazy blue eyes met hers, still full of amusement. And speculation. "The one lookin' for a husband."

"That's right," she said briskly, glad to be finally getting somewhere. "I'm here to—"

"Interview me. I guess that goes both ways, does it?"

"Of course. I'll be glad to answer any questions you still have."

"The only question I have," he drawled, "is what kind of a woman advertises for a husband?"

It shouldn't have surprised her: she'd heard it a hundred times by now, phrased a hundred different ways. Yet, for some reason, it always annoyed her. "Not much different from the kind of man who answers her," she replied more sharply than she'd intended. "Are you having second thoughts?"

He gave a snort of humorless laughter. "I've had nothing *but* second thoughts ever since I let my grandfather talk me into this."

Dani looked at him sharply. "Are you telling me you didn't answer my ad on your own initiative?"

"Buster thinks I need a wife. He saw your ad and figured this was my big chance."

"And he convinced you to answer it," she said with a frown, trying to calculate the implications of this little twist.

"He answered it. By the time I found out what he was up to, I..." He hesitated, then shrugged. "Although I'm almost tempted to give it a try. Can't be any worse than marrying for love." He gave a rakish grin. "And besides, having a wife around does have *some* compensations."

"Really?" Dani's eyes narrowed slightly, hearing something in his voice she wasn't sure she liked. "Such as?"

"A meal on the table now and again, if you're lucky. Clean clothes. Clean sheets. Maybe even *warm* sheets..."

To her annoyance, Dani flushed slightly. It wasn't the first time she'd heard variations on *that* theme, either, but for some reason she'd convinced herself it wouldn't be a problem here. So far, all the instincts she'd come to depend on over the years were failing her miserably!

"There's a name for what you're looking for, Mr. Montana. And it isn't *wife*." She dropped the shoes to the floor and rammed her wet feet into them. "I don't really think it's necessary for us to continue this discussion, do you? I was under the mistaken impression that you were serious about finding a wife. Obviously what you're looking for is a combination servant-mistress. And I'm sorry, but I'm not in that business."

A faint flush swept across his sun-browned features. His eyes narrowed, anger vying with some other emotion in their depths; regret, maybe. Or weary despair. "Just what the hell were you expecting," he grated, "roses and romance? Promises of undying love?"

His anger took her by surprise. She thought of the brief, impersonal details he'd given about his marriage and divorce, found herself wondering suddenly what kind of pain had been inflicted on him six long years ago, what dreams destroyed. There was still a rawness to the wounds. That was obvious. And, maybe because she understood a little too well about things like that, it made her pause. "No. I guess not. It's just that I'd hoped..." *Hoped what?* she asked herself brutally. You were hired to find Caroline a husband, not a fairy-tale ending, too.

"Love doesn't exist," he said harshly. "The best you can look for is that you don't wind up hating each other too badly."

Dani just stared at him, feeling a little shiver wind down her spine. My God, she found herself thinking, what kind of hell has he been through? "There's got to be something between love and hate," she whispered.

"You really want to know what I'm looking for?" he said with quiet savagery. "I want someone to help me raise my daughter the way she should be raised. I want someone who'll love this damn land as much as I do, who'll trust me to make something of it. Someone who won't be nagging me to sell and move to Vancouver when a late blizzard kills a quarter of the spring calf crop, or wolves bring down my best mare and her foal. Someone who'll work right there beside me, piling up straw bales when the creek comes up in the spring and threatens to take out the barn, or twenty cows decide to drop their calves early and we're out there in five feet of snow, trying to keep them alive."

Jake heard the intensity in his own voice but suddenly didn't care. "I want someone who can be cooped up here with four men and a kid during a three-day blizzard and still smile, someone who'll stand outside with me when it's twenty below zero to look at the stars just because they're so damn beautiful. I want someone here at night when I'm finished work, someone warm and soft and feminine who'll bring me hot coffee and rub my shoulders and tell me all about her day.

"I want somone to talk with, laugh with, share things with. And yeah, if she'll help with the laundry and the cooking and the cleaning and a thousand other things, that would be great, too, because running this place isn't any picnic, lady!"

The silence was absolute. Dani was staring up at him, her eyes unreadable. A rumble of thunder made him glance at the window, and Jake was surprised to see the sky dark with clouds. A few spots of wind-tossed rain hit the glass as another mutter of thunder rumbled down the valley. And suddenly he felt very weary, tired of baiting her.

"In a few minutes it's going to be coming down like there's no tomorrow," he said quietly. "That road out to the highway gets pretty bad when it's wet. If I were you, I'd leave while the leaving's good."

For a moment Jake thought she was going to say something. Then she nodded, expression thoughtful. "Yes, I suppose I'd better. I—" She gazed up at him, a frown tugging her brows together. But whatever she'd intended to say, she changed her mind and simply shook her head. She walked toward the door and picked up her briefcase. "Never mind. It's probably better this way. I'm sorry to have taken up your time, Mr. Montana."

Jake frowned. "What about you?" he asked. "What are you looking for?"

"Me?" She glanced around. "I—I honestly don't know. Caring, I guess. Honesty."

"And love?" He smiled, surprising himself with the question. "What about love?"

"No." The frown was back. She may have sighed. "I don't believe in it any more than you do, Mr. Montana. Certainly not enough to risk marrying for it."

She stood there for a moment or two longer, seemingly lost in thought. Then she shook herself free of whatever memories had ambushed her, and pushed the door open. "Goodbye, Mr. Montana."

"Yeah," he murmured, frowning slightly himself as he watched her leave. For half an instant he was tempted to call her back—why, he had no idea—but he waited a moment or two too long and then she was getting into her car and it was too late.

Too late for what? There was nothing left for either of them to say. But for some reason watching her leave gave him an odd feeling, half regret and half anger, almost as though he were letting something valuable slip through his fingers without even knowing what it was.

He watched Dani's car disappear through the spitting rain, then turned away from the door with a soft oath. To hell with it! He'd been ruder than he had needed to be; he would admit that. Ruder than he had *intended* to be. He couldn't remember the last time he'd had an outburst like that. She'd caught him off guard and something had just broken loose, something that had been festering away inside him for God knows how long. But, rude or not, it was too late for apologies now: Dani Ross was gone, and she wouldn't be back. And all of Buster's eloquent attempts to find him a wife had come to nothing.

Two

———

"Gran'pa, we have gotta do some of this laundry." Hands on hips, Cassie frowned as she surveyed the mountains of dirty clothes surrounding her. "It's gonna take a zillion loads at least to wash all these things!"

"I know, honey," Buster said. "But we can't use the machine until your daddy says it's okay. Although I guess I could pull it out to see if that danged hose is—"

"Like heck you will," Jake said, looking at his grandfather sternly. He'd caught the tail end of their conversation as he'd come through the door. "You know what Doc said about resting that hip. Remember what happened a couple of months ago when you got it into your head to change that truck tire. You want to go through all that again?"

"Not the same thing at all," Buster muttered grumpily. "I ain't gonna use my danged *hip* to pull that—"

"Buster, I swear I'll tie you down if I have to!" Jake drew himself up to his full six foot two and glared down at his grandfather.

Buster glared right back, not giving an inch. "Don't you try to bully me, youngster," he snapped, faded blue eyes sparkling with fire. "I raised you right outta diapers, and don't you forget it! I may be old and crippled and more of a nuisance than proper help around here, but I can still pin your ears back if I need to."

Jake backed down, fighting a smile. Looking properly contrite, he muttered, "Sorry. I didn't mean to mouth off. It's just that I worry about you."

Buster gave a snort, only half-mollified. "I was takin' care of myself long before you were even a smile on your mama's face. And I'll keep *on* looking after myself without any help from you!"

"I'm sure you will." Jake had to grin. Advancing years and a bad fall from a renegade horse two years ago might have crippled the old man's body, but they sure hadn't touched that fighting Greaves spirit.

He was harder to get along with than he had been before that spooked horse had left him nearly housebound, but that was to be expected in a man like his grandfather. Used to running Silvercreek Ranch himself, having grandson, hired hands and stock alike jump when he gave an order, it must have galled him half to death suddenly to be practically an invalid. He chafed daily at the restrictions the doctor and his own body put on him, paced the confines of the house like a corralled mustang, lashing out at anything that felt like a rope or saddle.

"I want to tape that hose coupling down before we try the machine again," he said. "Another day won't make any difference."

"But, Daddy!" Cassie's voice rose in dismay. "I won't have anything clean to wear to rehearsal tonight!"

Jake looked down at his daughter in surprise. Getting her into clean clothes was usually a battle. She flushed slightly, as though reading his mind, and kicked at a pile of dirty jeans.

"Is Robby Jacobsen in this play?" he asked innocently.

Cassie shot him a fierce look, as though suspecting him of laughing at her. He kept his expression carefully blank, and after a moment she nodded. "He's a troll."

There was an expressive snort from Buster's direction, and even Jake had to smile. "Tell you what, sweetheart. I figure that coupling should hold for at least one load of laundry. Why don't you pick out what you want to wear tonight, and we'll get it washed for you one way or another."

Cassie's face cleared and she dived into the nearest pile of clothes, found what she wanted and presented it to Jake. "Can I go now? Jesse said he was gonna let me help him build new roosts in Grand'pa's henhouse."

"'Going to'—two words," Jake told her patiently. "Is that project for Ms. Wilson finished?" Cassie's expression clouded over, but in spite of himself Jake had to smile. "I guess if Jesse needs your help, half-pint, the project can wait."

"Thanks, Daddy!" She was gone in a blur of denim, her shout of exuberance hanging in the air long after she had vanished.

"You spoil her somethin' awful," Buster said congenially.

"And you don't, of course," Jake retorted. "She's got you wrapped around her finger like a piece of string."

"Hell," Buster said with a sigh, "she's got us both wrapped around her finger, let's face it. I never was much at discipline—you're living proof of that. Never did listen to a damn thing I said. Even when it was for your own good." He gave Jake a sidelong look. "Like this Man-Hunters stuff, f'instance."

"I wondered when you'd get around to bringing that up." Jake tossed an armload of clothes into the washing machine and added the detergent.

"Wasn't right, sending her off like that," Buster muttered. "I shoulda been the one talkin' to her. After all, I was the one writin' the letters and fillin' in the forms."

Jake shut the lid with a bang and turned the machine on. "And I was the one who told you not to, remember?"

"She didn't say nothin' about coming back?" Buster asked hopefully.

"No." He said it roughly, annoyed to feel that lingering sense of regret shoot through him again. "And you're not to get in touch with her, hear? It's over!"

Buster gave him a mildly hostile look, then turned and walked away, leaning heavily on his cane but still managing to put enough offended dignity into his retreat to make Jake feel guilty. He muttered an oath under his breath and grabbed the mop from the corner.

Somehow, considering the way things had been going all morning, he wasn't even surprised when the hose coupling flew off about twenty minutes later and emptied the entire tub across the freshly mopped floor again. It was, he decided with philosophical calm, fit punishment for a man who had managed in the span of one short morning to shout at his daughter, hurt his grandfather's feelings and drive off a very attractive woman who had offered a unique, if potentially troublesome, solution to his problems. Maybe the universe was trying to tell him something....

He was still contemplating this some time later when he happened to glance out the open door to see Dani Ross striding up the lane. She was carrying the expensive shoes with the three-inch heels she'd been so proud of and was stomping through the mud and puddles of rainwater in her stocking feet, her expression as thunderous as the clouds roiling above her.

As she got closer, he could see she was soaked to the skin. Her elegant cream-coloured jacket hung from her shoulders like a wet towel, the matching skirt wrinkled and spattered with mud. The off-white blouse he'd figured must be silk clung to the surprisingly lush contours of her breasts like wet tissue paper, so transparent he could see a delicate filigree of lace under it. Her hair was plastered to her scalp and neck, and as she stalked through the last big puddle and up the steps to the back door, it was all he could do to keep from laughing out loud.

He pushed the screen door open and held it for her, and she stalked by him. "Couldn't stay away, huh?" he asked with a grin.

"My car," she said through her teeth, "is about two miles up that stretch of moose wallow you laughably call a road, buried to its axles in mud. I not only managed to put it in the ditch, I knocked down a fence post, wrapped a hundred feet of barbed wire around the grille and nearly hit a cow!"

For a moment Jake thought she was going to burst into tears. She was pale and obviously shaken up, and he looked down at her in concern. "Are you all right?"

"*I'm* fine," she almost wailed, "but my car's nearly a write-off. It stopped raining, so I decided to walk back here and then it started pouring again and—" She stopped abruptly and looked around the room as though just aware that she was standing in about two inches of warm, soapy water. "Oh, no, not again." Then, to Jake's astonishment, she broke not into tears but into gales of laughter.

Even Jake had to smile after a moment or two, gazing at the chaos around him. The piles of dirty laundry rose from the flood like waterlogged islands.

"I know it's not funny," Dani managed finally. "But it's obvious neither of us should have gotten out of bed this morning!"

He held up the roll of duct tape and grinned. "It's fixed for good this time. That thing's on there so tight you'd need a blowtorch to get it off."

She smiled. "You and my dad would make a good pair. He says you can repair just about anything in the world with a wrench, a hammer and a roll of electrical tape."

It was a good smile, Jake found himself thinking. Like her laugh, it fit her mouth easily, as though she smiled a lot. It was a good mouth, too. Generous and lushly curved. Like the rest of her. In fact, even soaked to the bone, her hair all wet and with black smudges under her eyes where her makeup had run, Dani Ross was one good-looking woman. Funny he hadn't noticed that before. All he'd seen earlier had been the slick big-city packaging: the expensive, dressed-to-succeed business suit, the eelskin briefcase, the brisk professional manner. But without all that, she looked surprisingly defenseless. And very much a woman.

He was looking at her, Dani thought, as though he'd never set eyes on her before. No, not just looking at her. *Seeing* her. And with a faint but unmistakable expression deep in those ridiculously blue eyes that told her as clearly as words that he liked what he saw.

Which was utterly crazy. She felt—and undoubtedly looked—like something left on a beach at low tide. She was wet and muddy and cold, and he didn't even want her here—so if he was looking at her oddly, it was probably just badly disguised annoyance at having her turn up again.

"You're cold." He said it quietly, so quietly that she glanced up, not certain he'd spoken at all. "You're shivering."

It surprised Dani to realize that he was right. Another chill ran the length of her spine. She shivered again and looked up at him with a rough gasp of laughter. "I'm wet."

"Damn." He laughed, giving his head a rueful shake as though bringing himself back into the present. "Sorry. Here—" He opened the dryer door and pulled a towel out before it had stopped tumbling. "This should be dry. I managed to run a load through before the hose came off."

The towel was thick, dry and warm, and Dani dried her face gratefully, then started rubbing her soaked hair. "If you can call a tow truck, I'll—" She stopped as Jake started to laugh. "What's so funny?"

"The nearest tow truck is fifty miles away, and they don't make house calls. Not this far out."

"But how do you get your car into the service station if it breaks down?" she asked incredulously.

"Out here you either fix it or shoot it." He grinned at her expression. "We might be able to get it out using the winch on the 4X4. If that doesn't work, I'll take the tractor out. And if *that* doesn't work, we'll just call the rental company and let them worry about it and I'll drive you into town. The guy who runs the garage is a friend of mine. He'll lend you a car to drive to Williams Lake where you can rent another one."

Dani winced. "I had no idea it was going to be so much trouble. In Toronto all I have to do is call the Auto Association, and in ten minutes I'm on my way. I'm sorry."

Jake's grin was lazy and relaxed. "Don't worry about it. Part of being a good neighbor is lending a hand when it's needed. And just to show you what a good sport I am, I won't even say anything about city women who drive up into country like this in white business suits and three-inch heels."

Dani managed a wry smile. "I appreciate your self-control. Because I *do* know better—I'm a country kid myself." His eyebrows rose and she laughed. "I know, I know! It's hard to believe. But under this Alfred Sung label beats the heart of a Saskatchewan farm kid. I guess ten years in the city have worn the edges off some of my country survival skills."

"Then I guess I won't write you off completely," he said with a husky laugh. "Anyone with country in their blood can't be all bad."

"I'm surprised you—" She glanced up, laughed and suddenly found the words spinning out of her mind like bright pieces of paper on the wind as his eyes met hers.

She had no idea of what she'd been about to say, seeing things in that look she hadn't seen in a man's eyes for years. Or maybe she'd seen it, she found herself thinking dazedly, but simply hadn't acknowledged it, hadn't *wanted* to acknowledge it. There was approval there, and admiration, but it was the underlying essence of pure, unmistakable sexual awareness that made her heart give an erratic little beat. It was the look a man gives a woman when he has just become aware that she *is* a woman, and to her astonishment, Dani felt herself blush.

She looked away, suddenly awkward, and found herself thinking inanely that the room had surely been larger a moment ago, that Jake himself hadn't been nearly so tall or so broad-shouldered or so near. His scent seemed to fill her nostrils, earthy and strangely erotic, and she sensed more than saw him move, shifting his weight restlessly like something large and powerful and wild.

"Come inside and I'll find something dry for you to put on," he said softly. "Shirt's no problem, but finding something for the bottom half won't be easy." His gaze drifted to her hips, lingered there long enough for Dani to feel the heat of another blush warm her cheeks. "I'll give you an old pair of my jeans. Maybe if we roll the legs up and run some rope around the middle to hold them up—"

"My suitcase is in the trunk of the car," Dani said quickly, trying to pretend this sort of thing happened to her every day. His suggestion made perfect sense, but the thought of discarding her clothes and prancing around in borrowed jeans struck her as just a little too intimate, all things considered. "If I can just hang my jacket up, I'll be all right until I can change into something...else." *Something of my own,* she'd nearly said, realizing just in time how idiotic it would sound. It was hardly a suit of armor she was clinging to so stubbornly, afraid of sudden vulnerability should she clamber out of it.

"At least get out onto dry land," he said mildly, nodding at the wash water still sloshing around their feet. "Coming in here to get dry was sort of like jumping out of a leaky boat into—"

"Daddy!" A small tornado hurtled into the room, nearly shooting out of control when it hit the wet floor. It careened to a stop inches from Dani, sending a wave of warm, soapy water over her bare feet. "Oops."

The tornado transformed itself into a small, very dirty child dressed in blue jeans and a cowboy shirt, wearing a grubby red-checked bandanna across the lower half of its face, outlaw fashion, and twin pearl-handled colt revolvers in crossed holsters low on its hips. Or what would one day be hips. At the moment the guns hung precariously somewhere between waist and knee, and the diminutive bandit gave them a hitch as they threatened to slide off altogether.

Dani stared down at the apparition, speechless. It looked up at her, and she realized that under the bandanna and dirt was a blue-eyed, tousle-haired little girl who was the spitting image of the blue-eyed, tousle-haired man standing beside her. "Hello, Cassie."

The big blue eyes blinked. "How'd you know my name?"

Dani smiled. "I know all sorts of things about you."

"How old am I?"

"Six."

"Nearly seven."

"Barely six," her father said. "And what are you doing roaring around in that getup? I thought you were helping your great gran'pa."

"I am!" she said indignantly. "He told me the most help I could be was to go play."

"Figures," her father said with a snort.

"Dale Anderson called and said the fence is down by Big Spring Creek and the cattle are wandering out on the highway."

"Damn it!" Jake wheeled around, snatched a dusty Stetson up and settled it over his pale, wind-tangled hair. He started toward the door, then paused to look at Dani. "Can you operate one of these things?" He jerked his head toward the washing machine.

"Of course I can."

"Good." He grinned then, a coaxing grin full of good humor and teasing. "Be a real sweetheart and run a couple of loads through while I'm gone, okay? And if you find anything that catches your fancy and might fit, put it on. It might be a while before I get back with your suitcase."

"Montana!" Dani stared at him in disbelief.

The grin broadened into sheer devilry. "You're looking for a husband, aren't you? Well, consider this a test of your domestic skills, honey. Do good, and maybe I'll marry you."

"*I'm* not the one who's—!" But she was sputtering into thin air. The screen door slammed and she was left alone, up to her ankles in water, wet hair dripping down the back of her neck and every stitch she had on soaked through. "This is the *craziest* place I've ever seen in my life," she whispered, staring around her. "The man doesn't need a wife. He needs a fairy godmother!"

"I can do it."

Dani had momentarily forgotten Cassie. She glanced around to find the pint-size outlaw struggling with the mop and bucket, and suddenly had to laugh. "Here, I'll give you a hand. I'll mop. You follow me with the bucket."

Between the two of them, it didn't take nearly as long as Dani had expected. It was scarcely ten minutes later that she set the bucket aside and turned toward the dirty laundry. "Okay, let's get this stuff washed. Let's start with—" She gazed around the room, feeling her heart drop at the immensity of the job ahead. "Good grief. Everything you own must be in here!"

"Almost," Cassie said cheerfully. "The danged washin' machine's been busted for nearly two weeks an' Daddy's been too busy to fix it. Gran'pa couldn't fix it 'cause he ain't s'posed to move heavy stuff on account of his bad hip, so we just been wearing the same stuff over an' over." She pulled the bandanna down and grinned at Dani. "It's great. Nobody hollers at me for gettin' my clothes dirty this way!"

Dani gave a sputter of laughter, already in love with Cassandra Jean Montana. It was too bad Jake's mind was so solidly made up about this. Two hours ago she'd been ready to write him off as a lost cause, but she was starting to suspect that her instincts had been right all along and that he *would* make Caroline a good husband, the kind of husband she'd secretly been hoping to find for her client all

along. And God knows, she thought as she surveyed the
battle-scarred laundry room, from what she'd seen so far the
biggest favor anyone could do for Montana was to find him
a wife. Whether he agreed or not!

"You're sure wet," Cassie suddenly said.

"As a matter of fact I am." Dani opened the dryer and
pulled out an armful of warm clothes. "Your dad said there
might be something in here I could put on. How about
helping me look?"

It was nearly twenty minutes later that Dani stepped out
of the small bathroom off the laundry room, dry and infi-
nitely more comfortable in a pair of men's jeans and a soft
denim shirt. Both were miles too large for her, but after
she'd taken a tuck in the waistband of the jeans and secured it with a safety pin, then rolled the pant legs and the
shirtsleeves five or six times, they were serviceable. She'd
stripped to the skin and had toweled herself thoroughly dry,
then had washed the smudges of mascara from under her
eyes and had loosely combed her wet hair with her fingers.
It was going to dry in a more authentic version of the "casual" look than her stylist had ever counted on, but that
couldn't be helped.

Arms laden with her own wet clothing, she turned the
corner and nearly ran into a broad male back. The man gave
a startled oath and turned awkwardly, leaning heavily on a
sturdy cane.

"I—" Dani fumbled with the bundle of clothes and held
her hand out. "I'm Danielle Ross, ManHunters Incorporated. And you've got to be Mr. Montana's grandfather,
William Greaves." He was staring at her in astonishment,
taking in her dripping hair, the oversize man's shirt, her bare
feet. Dani felt herself blush again, wondering in despair why
the menfolk of Silvercreek all seemed to affect her this way.
"I, uh, my car went into the ditch and I had to walk back in
the rain, and Jake—Mr. Montana, that is—said I should
find something dry to wear while I did the laundry, so—"
She frowned. "I'm not *really* doing the laundry. I'm just

waiting for—well, I *am* doing the laundry, but..." She stopped. "Maybe I should start again from the beginning."

"I don't think it would help." His eyes were blue, set in a face weathered to the texture and color of fine leather. He was still a handsome man, his features even and straight, and it took no imagination at all to see where Jake had gotten his rugged good looks. They both had the same eyes, the same strong chin, the finely curved mouth. And the same beguiling, half-shy smile. A large sun-browned hand took hers in a firm grip and held it warmly. "Damned if I know what's going on, Ms. Ross, but around here that's just normal. Jake said you'd left."

"I did." She gave a rueful laugh. "Fate seems to have decided otherwise, Mr. Greaves. Although in a way I'm glad. At least it's given me the opportunity to finally meet the man I've been corresponding with all these months."

"Call me Buster," he said with an embarrassed smile. "I guess Jake told you all about it, huh?"

"Just that you were the one who wrote the letters, and that he doesn't seem to really want a wife at all."

"Jake doesn't know what's good for him," Buster grumbled. "But with both of us talkin' to him, he—"

"Mr. Greaves—Buster." Dani held up a restraining hand. "It wouldn't be fair either to your grandson *or* to my client to pursue this. The decision has to be his, and it has to come from the heart. I won't risk my client's future happiness on anything less. Or Jake's, either."

Buster gave a thoughtful grunt. "This client of yours— you serious about finding her a good husband?"

"Very serious," Dani said quietly.

"You won't do much better than Jake." His eyes held hers. "I know this sounds like an old man's bragging, but it's God's truth. He's a good man."

"I don't doubt that, Buster. But—"

"What about you? You married?"

Dani had to laugh. "No, I'm not."

"Got anyone in the wings, so to speak?"

"No," she replied with a tolerant smile.

Buster nodded, his eyes sharp. "You like roast chicken?"

"Why?"

"You might as well stay for supper." He said it a little too guilelessly. "Better hang them wet things up, too. You can iron 'em later. Get 'em all fresh and pretty-looking."

Dani laughed. "Buster, I'm not in the market for a husband any more than Jake's looking for a wife. *I'm* the professional marriage broker here, remember? You just stick to grandfathering."

Buster's face broke into a sly grin. "Can't fault an old man for trying, can you?"

"Gran'pa! The calves are in the garden again!" Cassie hurtled between them, followed closely by a leggy yellow hound that skated wildly across the wet floor like a hockey player diving after a loose puck. The screen door flew open and slammed closed again. Seemingly unfazed, Buster wheeled around and started for the door himself, limping badly.

"Hold it!" Galvanized into action, Dani pounced on him. "You go back to roasting that chicken," she said firmly, "and I'll help Cassie with the calves." She took two steps toward the door, then looked around at Buster. "Where *is* the garden?"

"Just follow the racket." Buster grinned, nodding toward the open door. From somewhere just beyond came the sounds of battle: calves bawling, dogs barking, and above it all, a bloodcurdling war whoop that made Dani wince.

The garden, or what was left of it, wasn't hard to find. The calves were the first thing Dani saw, about twelve of them galloping straight at her as though the devil himself was on their heels. They saw her and wheeled as one, mud flying from tiny hooves, eyes rolling. The dog came racing right behind them, tongue and ears flying, and pounding behind it was Cassie, trailing what looked like a willow switch and a stream of oaths that would have done a mule skinner proud.

The entire cavalcade made another thundering circuit of the garden plot before Dani could collect her wits to intervene. She managed to deflect enough of the calves out through the hole they'd made in the fence to defuse the entire stampede and the rest of the livestock and their hard-driving cowhand slowed to a panting lope. The dog gently herded the last of the calves out through the fence and Dani gave the garden a final despairing look before following them.

"Guess we showed *them*, huh!"

"Yeah," Dani said with a laugh, "I guess we did."

"I'll go tell Jesse they're out. They're s'posed to be in the corral, but the fence needs fixin'. Can you ride?"

"A horse?"

"Of course!" Cassie gave her a strange look, obviously wondering what else they could be talking about. "That's my horse over there in that pasture."

"The paint or the buckskin?"

"The paint. His name's Apache." Cassie beamed. "I'll let you ride him if you like."

"I appreciate that, Cass," Dani said quite truthfully. "But I doubt if I'm going to be here long enough. As soon as your dad gets my car out of the ditch I have to leave."

"Oh, that won't be till tomorrow," Cassie said confidently. "I heard Daddy talkin' to Jesse before he rode out to Big Spring Creek. Jesse said he'd look at your car right away, but Daddy said it'll have to wait till morning."

"Oh, he did, did he?"

"Yup. And my daddy's the boss on Silvercreek Ranch."

"Your daddy is a—" She glanced down at Cassie's trusting upturned face and swallowed the rest. "Well, I think we've done all the damage we can out here. Let's go in and get some of that laundry done."

"Holy jumpin' catfish," someone muttered behind her. "The old man's going to have a fit when he sees *this*."

Dani wheeled around and found herself face-to-face with a tall Native American youth who was frowning worriedly at the garden.

When she met his eyes, he grinned and shoved his hand out. "I'm Cochise." Her face must have betrayed her, because he gave a sheepish laugh. "It's Gordon Spotted Horse, actually, but the half-pint here took to calling me Cochise, and it stuck."

"He's an Apache," Cassie said proudly.

Cochise smiled patiently. "Blackfoot."

"This is Dani Ross." Cassie looked immensely pleased. "She's out here investigating Daddy."

"Interviewing," Dani corrected swiftly.

"Daddy's getting a new wife," Cassie went on, unperturbed. "And Dani's checking him out."

"Cassie, that's not—!"

"Hey, half-pint, was that you I heard swearing a blue streak out here a few minutes ago?" To Dani's vast relief, another young man joined them just then. He was perhaps a year or two older than Cochise, with a mop of brown hair and a round, pleasant face sprinkled generously with freckles. He held his hand out to Dani, honoring her with the most angelic smile she'd ever seen. "Hi, I'm Jesse James."

Dani couldn't stop the smile, and Jesse grinned, obviously used to this response. "Awful, ain't it? My dad's got a real sense of humor, but he doesn't have to live with the jokes."

"Dani Ross," Cochise said, introducing her. "A...friend of Jake's." His broad smile spoke volumes.

To Dani's intense annoyance, she felt herself blushing. "I'm here on business," she said quickly.

Too quickly. Jesse grinned in response, his eyes twinkling as he took in the undoubtedly familiar jeans and shirt she was wearing. "Sure is nice to meet you. It'll be nice having a woman around."

"*I'm* a woman," Cassie put in indignantly.

"You," Jesse told her, "are in big trouble if I hear you swearing like that again."

"It's no worse 'n what I've heard *you* say," she muttered defensively.

"She's got you there," Cochise put in with a laugh. "It's probably time we *all* cleaned up our act."

Jesse gave a nod of grudging agreement. "Wouldn't hurt, with that social services woman nosing around."

"Social services?" Dani looked at him curiously.

Jesse's face darkened. "Some hotshot government type, new in town, who figures Cassie's growing up under bad influences out here among all us men. She's been out here a couple of times, snooping around, asking the neighbors questions. She wants to take Cass away from Jake and put her in a foster home—at least until he can get his home life in order, as she puts it."

"Meaning until he gets himself married," Cochise put in with a snort. "I'm telling you, you'd have to go a long way to find a better father than Jake. And Buster, Jesse and me might not be the prettiest talkin' guys around, but we take better care of Cass than any foster home!"

Dani had been watching Cassie's face during this, saw the flicker of fear in the child's blue eyes, the pale, pinched look that settled on the small, dirty face. She smiled reassuringly and draped her arm around the girl's shoulders. "I wouldn't worry about it. I suspect it's a lot of bureaucratic hot air."

Cochise opened his mouth to say something, then snapped it closed again at a warning look from Dani. He nudged Jesse and inclined his head in Cassie's direction. "Yeah, I expect so. You stayin' long, Miss Ross?"

"Dani. And only as long as it takes someone to get my car out of the ditch or drive me to the nearest rental agency."

"Might be a while," Jesse said with no apparent guile.

"So I've heard," she replied dryly. "Come on, Cassie. That laundry's waiting."

"Okay." Cassie fell into step beside her with a happy smile. "Look, there's Gran'pa, and he looks real excited."

He did, indeed, Dani thought as she saw Buster waving frantically at them. "I wonder what's happened *now*?"

It didn't take long to find out. Buster met them halfway, his face screwed up with a frown. "I just got a phone call from Evelyn Ousterman, and her baby's on its way. Her husband Ollie's out with the truck and she needs a ride into town. I hate to ask you this, Ms. Ross, seeing you're sort of a guest, but would you mind kind of keeping an eye on things here until Jake gets back?"

"Of course I will, but should you be driving?" Dani nodded toward his cane. "Maybe it would be better if I—"

"I can drive fine," he said with a smile. "It's walking I have trouble with. Besides, none of the roads are marked, and by the time I draw you a map showing you how to find the Oustermans' from here, and then how to find the hospital, well . . ."

"Go." She reached down and deftly untied the white apron from around his ample middle.

"You know anything about roastin' chickens?"

"Mr. Greaves," Dani informed him with a laugh, "I can not only *roast* a chicken, I can pluck it and clean it first! Do you want dumplings or biscuits with it?"

"Biscuits!" he and Cassie chimed in.

They walked into the house together, through the back porch that acted as the laundry room, down a corridor and into the living room. It was the first real look she'd had at Jake's home, and she couldn't stop her exclamation of horror.

It was a big room, comfortably furnished with well-worn but serviceable furniture. Two big sofas bracketed the fieldstone fireplace that dominated one entire wall, surrounded by plenty of solid tables and overstuffed armchairs of the type that wrapped themselves around you after a hard day's work the way a good chair was supposed to. It was, undeniably, a man's room.

There was also an unbelievable clutter of coats and boots and other clothing, toys, books, magazines, dozing cats, tools and what looked like a lawn mower engine that some-one had torn apart. A cardboard carton stood near the fireplace, filled with a pile of gauzy fabric from which rose one soiled and bent angel's wing. The room looked like one of those advertisements put out by insurance companies to scare people into doubling their coverage, and she half expected to hear a sepulchral voice warning her that *this* could happen to her.

"It's kind of a mess," Buster said apologetically. "I was hopin' to get it straightened out some before you got here in case you got the wrong idea about us. We had a house-keeper until she quit about a month ago, but..." He shrugged, not needing to say more. "You sure you're going to be all right?"

"Buster, I live and work in the heart of metropolitan Toronto. I can handle just about any situation you can throw at me. Besides," she added with a careless laugh, "what else could possibly go wrong?"

"Dani! Gran'pa!" Cassie came tearing into the living room, her eyes wide with panic. "Gran'pa, my dog's sick!"

Three

Is he gonna be all right?'' Cassie looked up at Dani worriedly.

Dani nodded. Between them on the bed the yellow dog gently licked the four damp mewling pups cradled against her belly. Hardly an hour old, they squeaked and pushed against one another, already nursing vigorously.

"He'll be—" Dani laughed. "*She* will be fine. The pups are all fat and healthy, and Ranger was obviously born to be a mother." Hearing her name, the dog looked up, practically beaming with pride, and thumped the bed with her tail.

"Boy, is Daddy going to be surprised when he gets home!"

"No kidding." Dani looked at the untidy nest Ranger had made out of the bedspread on Jake's big bed. The new mother gave a huge yawn just then and stretched out with a sigh of exhausted accomplishment, body curved protectively around the mound of wriggling puppies.

Dani stood up. "Come on, let's leave her alone for a while. She's had a busy afternoon and needs her beauty sleep."

Cassie bounced to her feet, eyes sparkling. "Isn't it neat? We've never had baby puppies before! Miss Margaret had four kittens last year, but then Daddy took her to the vet and she can't have babies anymore." She followed Dani out of the bedroom and closed the door gently behind them. "Mrs. Ousterman's cat had *six* kittens in January. She phoned Daddy and said we could have three of them, considering they all looked like Thomas Hijinks. That's the black-and-white cat asleep in the wood box in the living room. So then Daddy took Thomas to the vet and now *he* can't have kittens, either."

She sounded so thoroughly disgusted that Dani had to laugh. "Let's go and check on your grandfather's chicken. It's about time to put the stuffing in and pop it into the oven."

Jake caught a tantalizing whiff of roast chicken before he was even in the house. He walked across the yard wearily, slapping the dust from his jeans, and wondered how anything so simple could smell so wonderful. The kitchen was empty when he walked in. He pulled off his Stetson and ran his fingers through his matted hair, sniffing appreciatively as he walked by the stove. He could hear quiet voices in the living room and headed in that direction.

It was the angel that caught his attention first. She was standing in front of the fireplace, hands folded serenely in front of her, dressed in a gown of mist and silver. Her wings shimmered in the firelight, and when she moved they cast a spray of sparkles through the air like fireflies. A torrent of golden curls tumbled to her shoulders, held back by a broad silver headband that supported a sturdy halo, and Jake found himself gaping at the cherubic vision that had once been his daughter.

She was smiling down at the woman sitting cross-legged on the rag rug in front of her, and Jake found himself staring at another vision only slightly less stunning than the first.

Dani Ross.

But a completely different Dani Ross from the half-drowned version he'd seen last, or the sleekly put together businesswoman version who had first arrived at his door. This one was wearing one of his shirts, the top three buttons undone, sleeves rolled casually back to her elbows. The collar gaped widely, revealing the smooth curve of her throat and shoulders, and the deep V of the front accented her small oval face and cat-tilted eyes. Her hair, which she'd worn in a deceptively casual look, must have cost a fortune at one of Toronto's top stylists, had dried to a becoming tangle of curls. Gone were the gold earrings, the expensive wristwatch, the makeup. Unadorned by anything but glowing skin, laughter and firelight, she was the most beautiful thing he'd ever seen.

She looked up just then, generous mouth still trembling with laughter, and her dark brown eyes met his full on. It was like running into a concrete wall and he blinked, shaking himself free of the spell. "I forgot all about you."

"I suppose you forgot to pick my suitcase up, too."

He winced. "I'll send Jesse out after it."

"The same way you told him not to bother rescuing my car until tomorrow?"

Her tone was light, but Jake caught the edge of impatience to it. Damn. How had she found out about that? He'd done it completely on a whim, one of those spur-of-the-moment things that has neither plan nor explanation. It had just seemed very important at the time that she not leave before he saw her again, and had a chance to talk with her. "It was a matter of priorities," he told her, only half lying. "I've got a corral fence that needs fixing, a duck pond that needs dredging and about a hundred other things that need doing. Your car sort of slipped my mind. I'll send him out with the truck after supper."

A frown flickered across her forehead, and she dropped her gaze. "You're right, of course," she said quietly. "You do have a ranch to run. I'm sorry." Then she smiled and held her hands out to display her handiwork on Cassie. "Well, what do you think?"

"She's beautiful." Jake looked around the room with a puzzled frown. "But what have you done with Cassie? You remember her, don't you—the ragtag little tomboy who was here earlier?"

"Daddy!" Cassie gave him a long-suffering look, then held one arm out to admire the trailing cascade of gauzy fabric. "*I* think it's beautiful too. We've been working on it for hours."

"That's not all you've been working on," Jake said with awe. He stared around the room, scarcely recognizing it. Cassie's toys had been picked up and tossed into the big wooden box Buster had built for her, and all the stray clothes, boots, mittens and coats had vanished. The dozens of books and magazines were now tidily stacked on one of the big coffee tables and the tools and pump parts he'd been intending to pick up for weeks were now in a cardboard carton under another table. Everything had been dusted and polished, and even the motley collection of sleeping cats that never seemed to move from one day to the next appeared more tidily arranged.

"I hope you don't mind," Dani said apologetically. "I don't usually walk into a stranger's home and tidy up, but I was helping Cass look for her ballet slippers and one thing kind of led to another..."

"Mind?" Jake gave a strangled laugh. "There's furniture here I haven't seen in years!"

"We chased the calves out of the garden," Cass said proudly.

"And did twelve loads of laundry," Dani added.

"Collected Gran'pa's eggs."

"Washed about two weeks' worth of dishes."

"Mrs. Ousterman had a baby boy, six pounds and I can't remember how many ounces, and Gran'pa helped it get born and *everything*!"

Jake blinked, shell-shocked by the barrage. "He did *what*?"

"An' Ollie Ousterman called and said Gran'pa is a *hero*!"

"Evelyn Ousterman went into labor early and called here for a ride to the hospital," Dani explained with a laugh. "But they were a couple of minutes too late and she had the baby in the truck in front of the emergency entrance. By the time the doctor got there, Buster already had the situation under control." She grinned. "When he asked Buster where he'd learned to deliver babies so efficiently, Buster told him he'd been delivering calves and foals for over fifty years and couldn't see what all the fuss was about."

Jake found himself grinning. He settled his hands on his hips and looked around him again, shaking his head. "Maybe Buster's right and I *do* need a wife."

"Mr. Montana," Dani said as she got to her feet, "you don't need a wife. You need a miracle!"

"I'm starved!" Cassie piped up.

"We'll eat as soon as your grandfather gets back," Dani told her, obviously having that under control, too. "Why don't you go upstairs and change out of your costume."

Jake gave his head another bemused shake as Cassie obediently headed off, and wondered what it would be like to have the household running this efficiently all the time. Eerie, he decided. Definitely eerie! "I guess that means I have time to clean up before supper." He looked at her with a grin. "Did you iron my blue shirt, honey?"

Dani's head shot up, and she had her mouth partly open for a succinct reply before she realized he was teasing her. His eyes danced above a rakish grin, just daring her. She smiled sweetly. "Of course, darling. It's hanging in your closet. Would you like me to run you a hot bath to loosen all those sore old muscles, or get you a drink first?"

"A drink would be nice," he said huskily. His eyes locked with hers, filled with a sensual promise that Dani somehow doubted was entirely feigned. "Bring it into the bedroom and let's see if we can't figure out some other way to loosen up these sore old muscles."

His audacity took her breath away. But Dani held that bold stare without so much as blushing, determined not to let him win that easily. "It'll be awfully rushed," she purred in the most seductive voice she could muster. "Let's wait until tonight, so we'll have hours and hours to do it just . . . right."

For a moment Dani wondered if she'd gone too far. Jake stared at her, his eyes glittering with a sexual hunger so vital it couldn't possibly be anything but real. Then, suddenly, he threw his head back and gave a long, easy laugh. "You win, buttercup! Any more of this and the only person I'm going to embarrass is myself."

Dani smiled, knowing she should be angry but finding that damn grin irresistible. "My blushing-violet days are long gone, cowboy. I grew up with four brothers and a father who adored my sister and me but saw no reason to pamper us just because we were girls. It was a matter of either learning to hold your own or being bullied half to death." Her smile widened. "I learned early."

His own mouth turned up in a responding smile. "And I'll wager dollars to doughnuts there's not a man alive who could take you on and come out a winner."

She was caught off guard. A shaft of old anger shot through her with no warning at all, and she let her gaze slip before she could catch herself. It always surprised her how sharp and raw that anger could still be, even after all this time. "Not anymore," she whispered.

She looked up and found him watching her with a thoughtful expression, almost as though he understood exactly what had happened. Maybe he did at that. Did he find himself being bushwhacked by the occasional stray memory, too? She smiled, somehow feeling closer to him in that instant than she had to any other man. It was a good feeling, yet a little frightening. It was unnerving to think that a stranger she'd met mere hours ago could hold the key to her innermost thoughts that way.

A door closed with a bang that made them both jump. Dani heard Jesse's voice, followed by Buster's, and Jake smiled. "I'd better take that shower. Clean shirts in the closet, you said?"

"And clean jeans in the chest by the door."

"You're spoiling me, honey."

"Enjoy it while you can. And, cowboy!" He turned to look at her. "I'd plan on sleeping on the couch tonight if I were you." He gave her such a wary look that she had to laugh. "Remember that stray dog you let Cassie take in two months ago?"

"That yellow thing? What's he done now?"

"*He* just had four puppies in the middle of your bed. For a man whose livelihood depends on knowing your bull calves from your heifers, cowboy, you're not too swift in these matters."

He swore quietly, raking his fingers through his tangled hair. "I don't need a wife," he groaned as he turned away and started walking wearily toward the bedroom. "I need a vacation!"

"I've never seen anything like it," Buster was saying down at the far end of the table. "I turned to her and said we were at the hospital and she sort of smiled and said, 'Oh, I think it's too late for that.' And the next thing I knew, I had my hands full of newborn baby boy!" He beamed at his rapt audience. "Ollie says they're going to name him William, after me."

Jake smiled around a forkful of roast chicken. It had been a long while since he'd seen his grandfather so animated and full of good humor. Everyone at the table was enthralled by the story, and Jake was strangely content to find himself ignored and able to enjoy his meal in relative peace. Mealtime at the ranch was usually half social, half business, the only chance all of them had to get together. He, Jesse and Cochise would plan the next day's work while Buster and Cassie argued over whose turn it was to clear the table. Cochise would start teasing Cassie, then pretty soon Jesse and Buster would jump in on one side or the other, and within minutes they'd all be involved in a noisy, good-humored free-for-all. It was a definite treat to be able to concentrate on what he was eating for a change.

Which was, by anyone's standards, some pretty fantastic cooking! It was Dani's handiwork, obviously: a fat chicken stuffed with an apple-and-wild-rice concoction that was out of this world, potatoes mashed with butter and milk, pale, rich gravy, carrots and parsnips cooked together in a but-tery ginger sauce, and mouth-watering biscuits. He wasn't the only one enjoying it, either. Cochise and Jesse were packing it away as though they never expected to get fed again. And even Cassie had cleaned her plate twice.

As it had constantly that evening, his gaze drifted down the table to where Dani was sitting. She was between Cassie and Buster, both of whom had obviously adopted her, and Cochise hadn't taken his eyes off her all evening. Even Jesse, who had recently sworn off women after a tumultuous breakup with his girlfriend of six weeks, was being avidly attentive. Which wasn't entirely surprising. Women were a scarce commodity at Silvercreek Ranch. Especially ones as attractive as Dani Ross.

And she *was* attractive. Damn attractive, with those big eyes, brown one moment and gold the next, and that laughing mouth and slender little body that had more hid-den curves than a mountain highway. But it wasn't just that—the world was full of attractive women. There was something else about her that made it hard for a man to take his eyes off her, although for the life of him, Jake couldn't quite pin down what it was. Maybe it was that tumbling laugh that came so easily and naturally, or the way she made you feel calm and relaxed even in the middle of chaos, or the way she had of looking right into your eyes when you spoke to her, as though nothing else in the world mattered.

Or maybe it was just that she was so . . . female. She radiated a warm, feminine sensuality like heat from a stove, and he could feel his insides turning to butter whenever she was near. And it wasn't that deliberate, calculated sexuality some women had. Dani's was . . . soft. As natural a part of her as that marvelous smile, unplanned, uncalculated.

And damn near irresistible. When he was with her, it took every ounce of his self-control to keep from reaching out and running his fingers through her hair or touching her cheek. He found himself only half listening when she was talking to him, concentrating instead on her mouth, the moist sheen of her lower lip when she ran the tip of her tongue along it, fantasizing what it would be like to kiss her, to feel those lips open warmly under his. . . .

At that precise instant Dani turned her head. Those brown-sugar eyes met his straight on, and Jake distinctly felt his heart stop. He held his breath as her eyes widened very slightly, seeing God knows what in his expression. Whatever it was, it brought a very faint but unmistakable blush up from the neck of her shirt, and she looked away hastily, fumbling with her napkin.

That was smart! Jake swore at himself and concentrated on his supper. There were no two ways about it—he'd better get her car out of that ditch and get her the hell out of here before something happened they'd both regret. It was tempting; there was no denying it. All he'd have to do was play his cards right and she'd be his. For better or worse, till death did them part.

And then what? He didn't have a damn thing to offer a woman. Even if Buster was right in his estimate that she wouldn't have advertised for a husband if all she was looking for was romance, it stood to reason she expected more than she'd find out here at Silvercreek. Sooner or later, regardless of what she'd said, she'd expect love. And that was the one thing he couldn't give.

I'm not your man, he told her silently. *I don't know what it is you're looking for, Dani Ross, but I'm damn sure I'm not it.*

"She's really something, isn't she?" Buster gave Jake a speculative glance.

Jake gave a noncommittal grunt as he started gathering up the last dirty dishes from the table. Jesse and Cochise had cleared out before Buster could shanghai them into cleaning up, and Dani had taken Cassie into the living room to work on her costume. "If you don't hurry up, you're going to be late for rehearsal."

"Be a good chance for you two to talk, with me and Cassie out." Buster peered at his reflection in the window, smoothing his gray hair down with his palm. "How do I look?"

Jake grinned. "Like a million bucks. And you smell pretty, too."

Buster's cheeks turned faintly pink. "Thought I'd try some of that stuff you're always splashing on. Brings women swarming around you like bees around clover, so I figure it can't hurt an old coot like me. I courted your grandmother smelling like hay and horse sweat and she didn't mind, but..." He shrugged, then added swiftly, "not that I'm doing any courting, understand?"

"I understand," Jake drawled. "But a man could do worse than having a woman like Beth Wilson in his life."

"Wouldn't do a young buck like *you* any harm to have a woman in his life again, either." Buster picked up his old Stetson and put it on, adjusting it to a jaunty angle. "Come on, boy, admit it. You kind of like her, don't you? I watched you during supper tonight. You couldn't take your eyes off her."

"Make sure Cassie doesn't get into a fight tonight," Jake said mildly, carrying the dishes into the kitchen and dumping them into the sink. "Just because she's playing an angel doesn't mean she'll be acting like one. Last time, Frankie

Kortman went home with a black eye and his good shirt all torn up.''

Buster smiled reminiscently. "Serves him right for tellin' her she can't play ball just because she's a girl. Regular little Germaine Greer, she is. If she was old enough to be wearing a bra, she'd have burnt it by now.''

Jake had to laugh. "I think women quit doing that a few years ago. Just keep her under control, okay? Those boys are all going to have inferiority complexes if she keeps this up.''

"Hell,'' Buster growled with a good deal of pride, "compared with her, most of 'em are!''

Dani was sitting in front of the fire when Jake came back into the living room. She had her arms across one upraised knee, chin cupped in one palm, and was gazing into the flames. Jake strolled across and set a tray on the coffee table, then settled into one of the deep-cushiond sofas with a comfortable sigh.

She glanced up. Smiling, she reached for one of the big mugs. She added a generous splash of cream and took a sip. The coffee was rich and dark and perfectly brewed. "Buster and Cassie get under way?''

"Finally.'' Jake picked up the other mug, then leaned back and braced one foot on the edge of the table, resting the mug on his knee. He frowned very slightly, his thumb beating a silent tattoo on the mug. "I, uh, figure I owe you some kind of an apology for this afternoon. For just dropping you in the middle of everything, I mean, and then clearing out.''

"Yes, you do.'' Dani leaned back against the other sofa, mug cradled in her lap. "You know, for someone who doesn't *want* me here, you're not making much effort to get rid of me.''

He grinned lazily. "Maybe I'm just curious.''

"About?''

"Warts.''

Dani blinked. "Warts?''

"Well, maybe not warts exactly. Not physical ones, anyway. But I wasn't expecting a fashion plate, either. You're attractive, bright, funny—you must have your choice of men. So I can't figure out why you're advertising for a husband."

Dani's eyes widened. "But I'm not the—" She groaned, suddenly understanding. "Jake, it's not me who's looking for a husband! I was just hired to screen the applicants."

Jake stared at her. *"Hired?"* The word rang through the room, startling the sleeping cats.

"Jake, I'm sorry. It never occurred to me that you didn't realize..." She gestured helplessly. "I guess I just took it for granted that Buster had told you who I was and why I was here."

Jake gave her a dry smile. "He probably tried once or twice, but I kind of tuned him out whenever the topic came up."

"So you haven't seen any of the information I sent up?"

"I glanced through it, but there was no name mentioned, no picture, nothing to tell me that you weren't the lady involved."

"I did that for security reasons. Until I have the field narrowed down to two or three prospective husbands, I see no need for anyone to know who my client is—for her own protection. I sent Buster all the relevant information about her. But no name, no picture."

"So you're a marriage broker." He sounded bemused.

"This is my first and *last* foray into arranging marriages," Dani said with feeling. "I'm an executive recruiter—a headhunter. Companies hire me to find them the personnel they need."

"Only the position you're aiming to fill this time around is some woman's marriage bed."

"I guess that's one way of putting it."

"Well, hell," he growled, raking his hair back. "You mean I've gone out of my way to be nice and you're not even the—"

"Nice," Dani yelped. "You call what you've been *nice*?"

"Yeah, nice! I could have run you off with a shotgun."

"Instead of letting me do your laundry and clean your house and cook your supper and sew Cassie's costume and—and . . ."

"The dog," he said. "You forgot the dog."

"And chase the calves out of the garden, and—" She stopped, eyes narrowing. "You're laughing at me."

"No, no," he protested. "Keep going."

"I even *folded* your underwear, Montana. I could have just stuffed it into the drawer, but I folded it neatly and—"

"You didn't starch any of it, did you?" he asked innocently. "Damn, I hate starched underwear! Especially when I'm riding all day. You wouldn't believe how uncomfortable—"

"I wish I'd thought of it!" She continued to glare at him until, finally, she had to give in. "Damn you," she said with a quiet laugh. "You're insufferable!"

"So you're not the wife-to-be," he said with what could have passed for a sigh. "For a while there I had half a mind to give in and let you drag me to the altar."

"Then it's a good thing the truth came out before you got yourself in too deep, isn't it?" she said dryly. "Too bad all your efforts at being *nice* went to waste, though."

"No." Jake leaned forward and rested his elbows on his knees. His eyes were a hundred shades of blue and they held hers, lazy and warm. "It wasn't wasted, Dani," he said huskily. "Not a moment of it."

Dani's eyes widened slightly. Then she glanced away. The fire muttered and whispered, and he watched the reflection of the flames play across her face, finding himself, as he had so often that day, wanting to slip his arms around her. *You feel it too, don't you?* he asked her silently. *Chemistry, magic, curiosity—whatever it is, we both know it's not finished between us yet.*

"In a way," he said quietly, "I'm glad. When I finally get around to kissing you tonight, you'll know it's because of you, not because of any advertisement."

She gave him a quick, uneasy look, obviously not sure if he was teasing her or not. He smiled. "Thanks, by the way, for the laundry, the cleaning, the cooking, the costume making."

She watched him for a doubtful moment, then finally gave a quiet laugh. "You forgot the dog."

"So I did." He smiled down at her, loving the things the firelight did to her hair. "And the folding."

"Without starch," she assured him, still laughing. "I hate to admit this, but I had fun today. I can't remember the last time I cooked a meal like that. Usually I just toss something into the microwave or grab a salad at the deli. And I really enjoyed spending time with Cassie."

"I owe you thanks. It's not often she has someone all to herself. And I appreciate the work you did on her costume. When Beth Wilson phoned me last fall and asked if I'd like to enroll Cass in preschool classes a couple of times a week, I didn't realize I'd be making angel dresses."

"I scavenged some of it out of a box of Christmas decorations I found in the linen closet. I hope you don't mind."

"Best use most of that stuff has had in years."

"She was telling me that the entire class wrote *Heaven Loves Cowgirls* as a group project. It's a terrific real-life lesson in cooperation. This Beth Wilson sounds like a real jewel."

"Beth is a darn good teacher. This preschool thing is her idea. She put it together, got it financed, runs it—the works. Most of the kids around here are pretty isolated, especially when they're Cassie's age. Even if they've got brothers and sisters, they don't necessarily know how to relate to other kids very well. When they hit school age and suddenly have to interact with a whole classroom of strange kids, it can be hard on them." He grinned. "When Beth called me about enrolling Cassie, I don't think she knew what she was letting herself in for."

"It's probably been an education for them both."

"She's taken a special interest in Cass right from the start, giving her little assignments to build up her confidence, getting her interested in books, trying to show her there's more to the world than cowboys and horses." He smiled. "And teaching her to interact with other kids without hammering them every time there's a disagreement."

"Not to mention just *maybe* getting her out of jeans and sneakers long enough to see what being a little girl feels like."

"I'll believe *that* when I see it!"

Dani gave a quiet laugh. "I'll let you in on a little secret, Jake—mother nature will take care of it. I was the worst tomboy you ever saw until I was ten or eleven. It didn't happen overnight, but I gradually learned I could be a girl and still do all the things I loved, like baseball and hockey."

"Hockey? You? Come on! You look like you've always been the type for pink frilly dresses and paper cutouts."

Dani's laugh rose over the crackling of the fire. "I grew up in small-town Saskatchewan, my friend, where ice hockey isn't a sport; it's a sacrament. I was a goalie until I lost two front teeth—baby teeth, fortunately—and my mother put her foot down."

"That why you're not playing in the National Hockey League?"

"Hormones are why," she said wryly. "The year I turned fourteen I traded in my hockey skates and shin pads for figure skates and pink leg warmers. I set my sights on an Olympic gold for skating-singles instead of the Stanley Cup." She grinned. "Then I discovered that skating around with cute guys was more fun than practicing figure eights, and gave up that idea, too."

"Cute guys?" he asked with a pained look. She smiled and shrugged and Jake found himself watching the way the firelight caught tints of red in her hair. It highlighted the curve of her cheek and throat, and he traced her silhouette with his eyes following it to where glowing flesh and shadow merged at the V of the open shirt. Intent on their conversation, she had leaned forward, and the shirt gaped slightly, giving him a glimpse of the soft swell of her breasts, the cleft between them shadowed and tantalizing. It was innocently done, yet all the more provocative for its innocence, and Jake felt his mouth go slightly dry. "I'll bet you had them hovering around you like bees around clover," he said softly.

She looked at him quizzically.

"Cute guys."

As though just aware that he'd been watching her, she sat back, suddenly shy. Her hand went to the neck of the shirt instinctively, and she tugged it closed. "One or two, I guess," she said.

What in heaven's name was going on here? Dani asked herself desperately. This wasn't supposed to be happening. Not to her. And not here, with this man! It was utterly crazy, the way her heart kept doing cartwheels every time their eyes met.

She forced herself to ignore the way the firelight accented his strong, even features. "Your grandfather is quite a man. I'll bet he was hell-on-wheels before his hip started bothering him. Is it arthritis?"

Jake gave a snort. "Damn old fool was showing off his bronc-busting skills and got thrown. Shattered his hip—he's got more pins in him than a voodoo doll. Doctors say it's a wonder he's walking at all."

"It must be hard on him. On all of you."

"I think he's finally starting to face the fact he's never going to be able to do all the things he used to. But, yeah, it's been hard sometimes. He was all but housebound this past winter and it nearly drove him crazy. Nearly drove us *all* crazy." Jake grinned fleetingly. "He feels he isn't important anymore, that he's not contributing. He tries his best to run the house and take care of Cass but, well, you've seen her."

"This isn't any of my business," Dani said carefully, "but you said something about social services earlier...."

Jake's face hardened. "Some kid at a church picnic last summer started teasing Cass, and she whaled the tar out of him. His mother hit the roof. Not," he added grudgingly, "that I entirely blame her. Cassie was at fault. I admit that. The boy's mother started asking the other kids about Cass and didn't like what she heard." He frowned impatiently. "God knows, Cass has a temper like a firecracker, and I know she can swear like a deckhand given the right incentive, but so do most of the other kids her age. Difference is, she's a girl."

"And the boy's mother went to the social services people."

"She gave them an earful about Cassie's language, her fighting, the fact she goes around looking like a street waif half the time. Hell, I *try* to keep her cleaned up, but getting her into a bath or clean clothes is like hog-tying a calf, and some days Buster's just not up to it. If I'm here, fine, but if I'm not..." He shrugged. "Anyway, this woman from social services has decided I'm not a fit parent, that I'm not giving Cass the right *home environment*." The words were bitter, and he looked up, his narrowed eyes glittering, "I love my daughter, Dani. And I'll fight that woman right into the ground before she gets Cass away from me."

She put out her hand instinctively, and Jake's fingers folded tightly around hers, almost desperately. Suddenly she wondered what toll the constant worry was taking. What nightmares did he have? How many times did he wake up in the night and walk down to Cassie's room, just checking that she was still safe?

"What about a housekeeper? Buster said something about the last one quitting...?"

He gave a snort. "We've had five housekeepers in the past fourteen months. Damn good women, too, but Buster tries to straw-boss the household help like they're ranch hands, and after a few weeks they get fed up and quit. And then there's Cass.'' He grinned. ''She hates the feel of a rope or saddle on her. Things like making her bed and taking regular baths and wearing shoes aren't real popular with her. And Buster's no help. She'll get mad and go running to him and, of course, he takes her side. No woman in her right mind would want the job. I figure by now there's no one in the whole Cariboo who'd take it.''

''You're very honest, considering why I'm here.''

He grinned, his eyes catching hers and holding them. ''You've seen us at our worst. And you're still here.''

''No thanks to you,'' Dani protested with a laugh. She found herself tracing the strong contours of his face with her eyes, following the line of his neck to the wide sweep of his shoulder. He'd rolled his shirtsleeves up, and she could see the corded muscles in his tanned forearms, the faint sheen of golden hair along them. His hands were strong, too, square and competent. They were a working man's hands, nicked with scars, callused: hands that could wrestle a young steer to the ground for branding, repair a fence, gentle a nervous horse, stroke a sleeping child's cheek. Or make love to a woman.

She found the last thought disturbing, her mind suddenly filled with half-formed, erotic images, and she looked up to find Jake gazing down at her intently. Their eyes locked, and Dani felt an electric tingle shoot through her, wondering if he'd been watching her all this time. Wondering what he'd seen on her face . . .

Four

A pine knot split, hissing, and the air was suddenly pungent with burning pitch. Jake drew in a deep breath, hauling his mind firmly back from the decidedly erotic fantasies it had been weaving. A silver star lay by his foot, and he bent down to pick it up. When he slid out of the chair and onto the rug beside Dani, it seemed a perfectly natural movement, though he winced slightly as muscles stiffened from riding all afternoon twinged. Stretching out on his side, he braced himself on one elbow and held the star out. "This something important?"

"Heavens, yes! We spent half the afternoon cutting these things out. I'm going to trim the—" She stopped. "Actually, I guess you'll be trimming the hem with them. I shouldn't have started something you'll have to finish."

"It's a bad habit, starting things you don't finish." He held her eyes deliberately, knowing she was thinking exactly the same thing he was. "You could always stay awhile." He didn't even know he was thinking it until the words were out, but for some reason they didn't surprise him. Nor, for that matter, did she seem surprised to hear them.

She smiled. "I have a job to go back to, remember?"

A lock of her hair had fallen forward, and he reached across and brushed it back slowly, the need to touch her too strong to ignore. Her hair was like silk, almost too fine to be real. Strands of it caught in the nicks in his work-roughened fingers, and he suddenly became aware of how delicate she was, how oddly erotic the contrast was between the feminine curve of her cheek and the uncompromising maleness of his own hand.

Carefully he drew his hand from her, knowing if he didn't now he never would. "I could always hire you as head of angel engineering or something. I need all the help I can get."

Dani laughed. Her eyes sparkled, meeting his in that half shy, half bold way that told him she, too, was aware that something was happening between them, unbidden and unexpected but not entirely unpleasant. He smiled at her, lazy and relaxed and quite content to simply enjoy whatever it was for as long as it lasted, and she smiled back.

Then her gaze slipped from his, a faint blush turning her cheeks pink. "I think," she said very quietly, "that I should get back to Toronto."

Jake didn't say anything. She reached out to take the star, and he caught her hand. It lay unresisting in his calloused palm, and he splayed his fingers, meshing them with hers. He looked up and found her face distractingly near. She was looking at their braided fingers, a small frown wedged between her brows. Her downcast lashes cast a scythe of shadow across each cheek, and he let his gaze move leisurely from feature to delicate feature, drinking in her feminine perfection.

Like every good tomboy, she had freckles, a spray across the bridge of her nose, so faint you had to be very close to see them. He studied the thrust of her cheekbones, noting the angle of her jaw and the firm little chin that he already knew from experience could be as expressive as words. Her lips were full and lush and slightly moist, and he stared at them in fascination, wondering if they could possibly be as soft as they looked.

She looked up just then, as wide-eyed as a deer. Her eyes were a rich brocade of browns and liquid golds, soft in the firelight. He could feel her breath against his cheek, could see the rapid flutter of her pulse in the hollow of her throat. Her skin was as smooth as cream, and he leaned forward without even thinking about it, almost but not quite brushing his lips against hers. Her fingers flexed convulsively in his, and she went motionless, eyes sliding closed, not even breathing.

It was one of those fragile instants in time that can seem eternal, and Jake let himself relax, drawing her sweet, unperfumed scent deep into his lungs. He could have moved his face that additional half inch that separated them, could have run his mouth down her cheek to hers and to the lushness he knew awaited him. And yet there was no urgency. He was completely content simply to savor the promise of the riches she held, knowing that this gentle, unhurried magic, whatever it was, belonged to both of them.

"I should go." It was just a whisper. When he said nothing, she looked up, eyes almost pleading. "My... my car. Were you going to look at it tonight?"

"It's late." Jake held her gaze evenly. "You could stay here tonight. Your suitcase is already here and there's plenty of room."

He heard her swallow. "You... could drive me to the nearest motel."

Jake took a deep, careful breath. "I don't suppose," he said softly, "that you intended that to mean what I'd like it to mean."

She seemed to be holding her breath. In the stillness he could hear a calf bawling somewhere. "And I don't suppose," she whispered, "that you meant that to mean anything but what it did . . . ?"

He brought his face down to hers, moving his lips lightly across her cheek. Her skin was soft and warm, and he had to fight to catch his breath. He felt torn apart, half of him wanting the sweet agony of anticipation to last forever, half wanting her naked in his arms, now, here, arching under him as he filled her, wrapping those long, slender legs around him and letting herself go as he ached to let go. He cupped her other cheek in his hand and nuzzled the downy spot under her ear.

She groaned softly and turned her face against his, her mouth seeking his. He kissed her lightly, sliding the tip of his tongue across her lips, coaxing them apart. She shivered and kissed him back, the tip of her tongue darting between his, gone before he could capture it. He cupped her face between his palms, thumbs stroking her cheekbones and then, finally, he settled his mouth firmly over hers.

She opened to him like a flower opening to the rain, and he kissed her slowly and deeply, savoring every warm, moist moment. His heart was drumming a tattoo against his ribs, and he felt the last tenuous threads of his self-control pull dangerously thin. Her tongue moved in sinuous concert with his, a slow, rhythmic dance keeping time with the heavy pulse of his own blood. It was as though she were already part of him, as though they shared the same blood, the same breath, the same bone.

How he ever managed to stop it there, he didn't know. It would have taken no more effort to have made love to her right then and there than it had to take that first kiss. And there had been a moment or two when he'd had no doubt that that's where things would have ended. But some old-fashioned sense of chivalry he hadn't even known he possessed made him draw his mouth from hers.

Her forehead rested against his cheek so that his face was buried in her hair. He kissed the top of her head, then pulled back so he could look down at her. "Dani?" he asked softly, not even bothering to say the rest.

"Oh, Jake..." She closed her eyes for a moment, then opened them again, her eyes searching his.

He nodded slowly and smiled. "Not mad at me for asking, are you?"

"Of course not," she whispered. "I'm just angry at myself for being so straightlaced. I never was any good at this kind of thing...."

"I'd say you were very good at this kind of thing," he murmured, giving her another quick kiss. Then, as her mouth responded to his, what started out as a simple kiss threatened to turn into something else altogether, and he gave a groaning laugh, easing himself away from her. "I think we should call it a night, buttercup."

She closed her eyes and nodded, her breathing uneven. "Good idea. A... *very* good idea."

"You're not really going to make me put on a coat, get the truck started and drive you fifty long miles to the nearest motel, are you?"

"I should." A smile played around the corners of her mouth.

"Well, you probably *should*," he teased. "Having you under the same roof all night is going to cause me some serious sleeping problems. But that spare bedroom upstairs has a lock you'd need dynamite to get through. You'll be safe. I swear it."

Her eyes sparkled with sudden mischief. "But the question is, will *you*?"

Jake smiled down at her and ran a fingertip slowly across her lower lip. "I'd like to think I won't be. I moved Ranger and her family to Cassie's room, and that's a hell of a big bed I've got in there all to myself. Plenty of room for two..."

She smiled wistfully and kissed his finger. "You'll never know," she whispered, "how tempting the offer is."

"But," he completed for her with a laugh. "The ubiquitous 'but.' I wonder how many times a man has had his hopes dashed with that one simple word."

It made her laugh, as it was meant to, and he kissed her swiftly on the mouth, then got to his feet. "I'm serious about that offer of a room. No strings attached."

Dani looked at him for a long moment, knowing she should be saying no, that the wise thing would be to drive that cold fifty miles to the nearest motel before things got any more complicated. "Oh, hell," she whispered, "why not? Besides, I want to hear how rehearsal went tonight."

"The rehearsal was great!" Cassie's eyes glowed over her glass of milk. She drank deeply, then licked at the white moustache around her mouth. "I was really good, wasn't I, Gran'pa? Ms. Wilson said I was the best heavenly angel ever!"

"She did indeed." Buster beamed down at his great-granddaughter. "Not one of those other kids even came close."

"Who wants more?" Dani looked around the table, holding up a plate laden with golden pancakes. "Come on, Jesse, I know you've got more room."

Jesse, caught with his mouth full, nodded vigorously and held his plate out. Dani slid another half-dozen pancakes onto it, wondering where on earth he was putting them. "Jake?"

Jake eyed the plate in her hand, then shook his head in defeat. "I can't."

"Hope you're planning on staying awhile," Buster said with a satisfied sigh as he pushed back his sticky plate. "You surely do know how to start a man's day off properly."

Dani, carefully avoiding Jake's amused gaze, looked down at Cassie. "How about you? Does the best heavenly angel in the Cariboo have room for one more?"

"No, thanks. I'll 'splode!" Cassie gave her a sticky grin. "I wish you coulda seen me, Dani. Everybody loved my costume. Even that dumb Robby Jacobsen said I looked nice, didn't he, Gran'pa?''

"Two or three times," Buster said with a chuckle. "That young lad's so smitten it's painful to watch."

"And how about Ms. Wilson?" Jake drawled, looking at Buster over the rim of his coffee mug.

"She invited Gran'pa to supper next week," Cassie spoke up promptly. "She said I can come, too, if I wanna."

"'Want to,' Cass—two words." Jake smiled lazily. "And I don't think your great-granddad needs a chaperone. Although..."

"Although nothin'," Buster growled, giving Jake a fierce look. "She's just being polite, that's all. Her way of thanking me for helping with the scenery last night."

"You were making sets?" Jake's eyebrows rose.

"Just hammered a couple of nails in, that's all," Buster muttered. He swept a ferocious glare around the table, daring anyone to argue. "This ain't a picnic, Jesse—finish them pancakes and get on out to work. You, too, Cochise. Ton of things need doing." Cochise and Jesse scrambled to their feet and headed for the door, grinning their thanks to Dani, and Buster glowered at Jake. "And what are *you* laughing at? You got spare time on your hands? I'll find something for you to do around here!"

Jake eased himself to his feet. "I'm going, I'm going!" He looked down the table at Dani, his smile broadening. "I promised Ms. Ross I'd try to get her car out of that ditch."

"You're not going, are you, Dani?" Cassie looked at her beseechingly. "You haven't seen Gran'pa's ducks or ridden Apache or seen my tree house or nothing yet. You can stay—Daddy, she can stay, can't she? And besides, you can't go till you've seen the play. It's only next week, Dani. You can stay till then, can't you? Please?"

"Oh, Cass." Dani knelt beside the girl's chair, smoothing a flyaway strand of silken hair. "Honey, I wish I could." To her surprise, Dani realized it was true. It was crazy, but in the space of barely a day she'd fallen in love with Silvercreek and everyone on it, including this sticky, wide-eyed little girl who was looking at her so anxiously. "But I just came out here on business, Cass, and now I have to go back to Toronto."

"But you don't *hafta* go back," Cass pleaded. "Gran'pa said you were out here to talk to Daddy about getting me a new mother, but I'd rather have *you*."

"Cass..." Dani looked around at Jake for help, but he was standing at the sink, hands on hips, staring out the window. "Cassie, I'm afraid it's a lot more complicated than that. And I'd love to see your play, but—" She stopped, sighing inwardly as she watched Cassie's face fall. "I have an idea—why don't you get your father to take some pictures? You can send them to me and—"

"It isn't the same and you know it!" Cassie flung herself off the chair and stormed toward the door, casting Dani a hostile look. "I thought you were different. But you're just like that lady from town who wants to take me away—she talks to me like I'm just a dumb little kid, too!"

"Cass...!" Dani started after her, then stopped. "I sure know how to handle kids, don't I?"

"Don't blame yourself, honey." Buster patted her awkwardly on the shoulder, then started clearing the breakfast dishes. "She doesn't usually let people get too close. I'm surprised she took to you right off, to be honest. She doesn't want to admit she's going to miss you, so she gets mad to cover her feelings. But she'll be okay in a day or two."

"She was right, you know," Dani brooded. "I *was* talking down to her. I used to hate being patronized by adults when I was her age, and now I'm doing the same thing."

Buster chuckled. "It's hard knowing what to do with them at that age. They're not grown up, but in a lot of ways they're wiser than Solomon. Jake was the same. And it gets a heck of a lot worse before it gets better. Remember when you was thirteen?"

Dani had to laugh, feeling some of her gloom lift. "I wouldn't go through that again for anything! I was the town's worst tomboy one minute and experimenting with my sister's lipstick the next. No one understood me. Every girl in class but me had breasts and my brothers kept teasing me about Lloyd Jenkins, the fat kid next door with all the pimples who used to follow me *everywhere*." Dani grinned. "He's now head of his own multinational corporation and richer than Midas, but back then he was the bane of my life."

Jake turned away from the window and laughed. "You got any of that tomboy left in you, or are you too much the big-city girl these days to go riding with me?"

Dani looked up in surprise, her hands full of dirty dishes. "Riding? I thought you were going to look at my car."

He settled his Stetson over a tangle of golden hair, then tipped it forward at a rakish angle so that his eyes were in shadow. "I will."

He looked like the hero of a thousand western novels, tall and lean, mouth canted in an *aw-shucks* grin guaranteed to melt the most skeptical feminine heart. But the glitter in his eyes was pure outlaw.

Dani took a deep breath. "Jake, I have to be in Williams Lake by two this afternoon to catch a plane."

"You'll be there."

"I—" She looked at the mountain of dishes stacked beside the sink.

"I can handle these," Buster told her calmly.

Dani's mind whirled, searching desperately for an excuse—any excuse—not to go. "I don't have anything to wear...."

Jake laughed. "The eternal cry of the female species. What you're wearing right now is fine." He nodded at her gray wool slacks. "You just have to ride him, not wrangle him."

Don't be such an idiot she told herself angrily. There was no reason *not* to go. "All right," she heard herself saying, wondering if she sounded half as nervous as she felt. "I, umm, want to put a sweater on though, okay?"

"Good idea." Jake gave a satisfied nod and turned away. He paused at the door, looking around at her. "You a beginner or an old hand?"

"I don't want to have to break him, if that's what you mean. But you won't have to tie me on, either."

"Tinkerbell," he and Buster said in unison. Jake smiled. "I'll meet you at the corral gate in fifteen minutes."

Up in the comfortably furnished bedroom where she'd spent the night, Dani stood by the window for a nervous moment and watched Jake stride across the yard toward the barn and corrals. He walked like a man with a mission in life, and Dani sighed.

She had a mission, too, and she should be getting on with it. Caroline Wainwright was sitting back in Toronto nervously awaiting the results of those fifteen interviews, and she was going horseback riding! The fact she was going with one of the candidates in no way excused it—Jake had already told her point-blank that he was out of the running.

She ran her brush through her hair, frowning at her reflection. Last night in front of the fire hadn't exactly been by the books, either. She was out here to *interview* the candidates, not audition them.

She had to smile at the thought. Strictly as an *audition*, last night could be said to have been very successful. Jake had proved himself to be thoroughly adequate in the charm department, *more* than adequate when it came to the fine art of gentle seduction, and as for his ability when it came to kissing...!

She fanned her warm cheeks with her hand, grinning at herself in the mirror. "Incendiary" might be an apt description. Just thinking about it made her heart beat faster, sent a shivery little tingle to a spot somewhere between her navel and her knees.

Damn it, will you stop this! She gave herself a mental shake and concentrated on getting ready. She simply finger combed her short hair and left it tousled, hummed and hawed about putting on lipstick, decided not to, put a swipe of eye shadow on each lid and immediately wished she hadn't. She wiped it off, frowned, put it back on. Two dabs of perfume later she was wishing she had told Jake no, and by the time she'd changed her sweater twice, her blouse once and had spent five full minutes agonizing over which earrings to wear, she was wishing she'd never left Toronto.

"This is ridiculous," she muttered to herself as she fussed with the collar on the white silk shirt she'd finally settled on.

So they'd kissed in front of the fire last night. So what! It had been one of those silly things that happens, a spark of sudden magic between a man and woman. The proposition that had followed had been perfectly normal, too, as forthright and honest as the man himself. He'd asked, she'd declined, he'd accepted her refusal like the honorable man he was, and that was all there had been to it. It was hardly the first time an attractive man had asked her to go to bed with him.

But that wasn't the problem at all, Dani reminded herself. It wasn't his asking that had frightened her; it was how close she'd come to accepting. It would have been the classic one-night stand, a night of pleasure shared by two people who would never see each other again, and she'd come *this* close to saying yes.

So no matter what she told herself this morning, last night hadn't been *just* another kiss in front of the fire. And Jake Montana, all six feet two inches of him, wasn't *just* another pretty face!

"I hate to admit this," Dani said over her shoulder, "but before coming up here, I didn't even realize there *were* ranches in the B.C. interior. I thought it was all mountains."

"You've been reading too many ski brochures." Jake ducked to miss a low branch on an old jack pine leaning across the trail. "One of the biggest cattle ranches in Canada is southwest of here. When people think of Canadian ranches they think of Alberta, but the Cariboo area has some of the best grazing land in the world.''

He touched his horse with his heel, and the big buckskin broke into an easy canter, bringing him up beside Tinkerbell. The chestnut mare shied playfully, but Dani ignored her, perfectly at ease in the saddle.

She rode like a natural, Jake noticed with approval, upright and loose, well balanced in the stirrups. Tinkerbell, although sweet-tempered, was spirited enough to keep up with Cherokee and enjoyed intimidating an inexperienced rider if she could get away with it. But she had quickly discovered that Dani wasn't going to put up with any of her usual tricks, and after a mile or two of shying at shadows and nipping under low branches, she'd settled down. She was trotting along now like a perfect show horse, ears pricked well forward, neck arched slightly, as though aware of the pretty picture she and her rider painted against the morning sky.

For his part, Jake found it hard to take his eyes off his riding companion. Dani was wearing a white shirt, collar turned up jauntily in the back to frame her face, and over it a bright red-knit sweater with satin appliqués down the front and across one shoulder. It was all but impossible not to notice other things, too. The way her taut little bottom fit the saddle just perfectly, for instance, or the subtle but unmistakable rise and fall of her breasts under the sweater.

Not a smart idea. His body responded a little too vitally, and he shifted uncomfortably in the saddle, putting his imagination firmly on hold. Cherokee gave the mare a nip that made her snort and dance aside, eyes rolling, and Dani laughed. She reined Tinkerbell back in and the two horses trotted side by side companionably.

''Glad you came?''

Dani looked at him and smiled, cheeks pink in the cool mountain air. ''You know darn well I am, cowboy. Don't fish for compliments.''

He laughed and brought Cherokee in close to the mare so that Dani's knee bumped his. "A man doesn't get away with much when he's with you, does he?"

"A man doesn't get away with *anything* when he's with me."

"That a friendly warning?"

"If it needs to be." She chuckled. "What are we talking about, anyway?"

"Beats me," he said, still laughing. "How did you sleep last night?"

"Like a baby."

"Have any dreams?"

"One or two."

"Was I in them?"

"Nope."

"You were in a couple of mine."

She gave him a lazy look. "I hope you enjoyed yourself."

"I did."

"Did I?"

"Yeah." He grinned down at her. "Join me tonight and find out why."

Dani gave a peal of laughter, flicking the reins against Tinkerbell's neck. The mare danced away, and Dani smiled across at Jake. "I admire your persistence, cowboy, but I'll be in Vancouver tonight, remember?"

"Your car's still sitting in a ditch waiting for me to dig it out, remember?"

They rode on in silence for a few minutes, then Dani reined the mare up and looked at Jake, suddenly serious. "I do have to get back to Vancouver tonight, Jake. I have an appointment with someone tomorrow morning."

Jake tugged his hat down to shade his eyes from the sun. He looked out across the rolling hills to the Cariboo Mountains, rising like a fortress across the east. Even with the sun on them they looked cold and dangerous. "More husband material?"

She nodded. "Stockbroker. I talked with him before I came up here."

"Good bet?"

"The best so far."

"I see." The words were clipped. He refused to look at Dani, continuing to stare across at the distant mountains as though just seeing them for the first time. Why the hell it should bother him, he had no idea.

"Next to you, of course."

It took him a moment to realize what she'd said. He looked at her sharply, fully expecting her to break into uproarious laughter at his expense.

But she didn't. Her eyes met his evenly, and she smiled. "I had a tough time believing it myself at first. But in spite of the fact that your life resembles an afternoon sitcom, you're the man I'm looking for."

He didn't say anything. A peculiar expression that Dani couldn't identify crossed his face, and she wondered what was going on behind those wary eyes. Tinkerbell tossed her head with a snort, pulling at the bit impatiently, and Dani loosened the reins. The chestnut moved into a walk, and after a moment Jake turned the big buckskin and fell into step beside her.

"That stockbroker in Vancouver has got everything going for him," Dani said. "He's wealthy, ambitious, smart. He has a waterfront home in West Vancouver, a ski condo in Whistler, a Porsche. But he's closing in on thirty, and he figures he should have a wife and the stable home life that clients expect from a man in his position."

"But he's too busy working his eighty-hour weeks to look for one."

"Exactly." Dani glanced at Jake, but he was staring straight ahead intently, seeming captivated by the view. "You, on the other hand, have none of those things. You have a home that runs on total anarchy. You have a semi-invalid grandfather, a daughter who thinks she's Huckleberry Finn and a washing machine you don't dare turn your back on."

Jake winced slightly. He looked at her, eyes unreadable in the shadow cast by his hat. "Is that the good-news part?"

Dani laughed softly. "No. The good-news part is that you're a decent, honest man with a strong sense of responsibility. If you gave your word to make my client the best husband you know how, you'd do it. Then there's my client herself. She loves children and animals, quiet afternoons in front of the fire with a good book, stimulating conversation. The stockbroker doesn't think he'd mind one child, but animals are out. Not with his antique furniture and Aubusson rugs. My client has a bright, inquiring mind, and there are times when she's almost childlike in her enthusiasm, especially about people. The stockbroker wants a sophisticated wife who can be the perfect hostess for his business dinners, but he's not exactly an intellectual."

Jake snorted. "And I am?"

"I've looked through your bookcases, cowboy. Your reading material runs the gamut from Nietzsche to Zane Grey, with a smattering of history, politics, New Age philosophy and agricultural science tossed in. You enjoy science fiction, mysteries, political intrigue, Shirley MacLaine and modern poetry. You're interested in everything from space colonization to wildlife conservation, and you subscribe to enough magazines to qualify for a library grant. So don't play the dumb hayseed with me, okay?"

He fought the smile, but it finally got the better of him and he laughed out loud, shaking his head. "Damn you're good!"

"Yes," she assured him, "I am."

"Got any more revealing insights into what makes Jake Montana tick?" He slid her a lazy glance, half teasing, half curious.

"Plenty. I've earned a reputation for being one of the best executive recruiters in the business. One of the reasons I'm good at what I do is because I've learned to trust my gut instincts about people. I can tell within the first ten minutes of an interview if the candidate is suitable for the position I've been hired to fill, and I'm rarely wrong." Dani looked at Jake seriously. "And my gut instinct tells me you'd make my client an excellent husband, Jake."

Then she gave a quiet, rueful laugh. "The problem is, you don't want the job. So it's between the Vancouver stockbroker and an accountant in Halifax." Jake didn't say anything; he just looked at her with that odd expression on his face again. Dani's eyes narrowed. "You *did* say you weren't interested, didn't you?"

He frowned slightly and looked away, gazing at the distant mountains. Dani reached out and caught Cherokee's bridle, reining Tinkerbell in sharply. Both horses jostled each other, but Dani pulled them up hard and looked at Jake. "You're having second thoughts, aren't you?"

A look of impatience flickered around his face, and for a moment Dani thought he was going to wrench Cherokee's head around and gallop away. Then he swore under his breath and pulled his hat off. He combed his hair back with his fingers and resettled the hat, then looked at her, his face guarded. "Let's talk."

He swung down out of the saddle before Dani could say anything. Dropping the reins in front of the buckskin, he turned and strode across to a giant jack pine that stood like a sentinel at the top of a gently sloping hillside. Dani dismounted thoughtfully and followed him, leaving the two horses grazing contentedly.

Jake was leaning against the tree, fingers jammed into the pockets of his jeans, eyes narrowed as he stared out across the sweep of rolling hills to the mountains beyond. Dani drew in a deep breath of the crisp, pine-filled air, feeling it tingle through her like fine champagne. She walked past Jake to the edge of the slope, drinking in the spectacular view as deeply as she had the mountain air.

"You want to watch them."

Dani looked over her shoulder questioningly.

"The mountains." Jake shrugged away from the tree and strolled across to stand beside her, nodding toward the distant rampart of rock serrating the eastern sky. "They get in your blood after a while. Spend enough time among them and you'll never want to leave."

And what about you? she found herself thinking. *How long does it take for a woman to get you in her blood and never want to leave?*

Five

I can't get over how clear it is. In Toronto air is something you look *at*, not through. A friend of mine says you don't breathe it as much as chew it up and swallow it."

Jake didn't take his eyes off the horizon. "Sandra, my ex-wife, hated them. The mountains, I mean. She was from a little pulp and paper town on the coast, so isolated there wasn't even a road in. The only way to get out was by boat or plane. She used to say the mountains around it reminded her of bars on a cage." He was silent for a while.

"She came out to the Cariboo to visit friends, and I met her at a dance. She was the most gorgeous thing I'd ever seen, and I guess I must have looked pretty good to her, too, because we wound up together for the weekend." His smile was faint and bitter.

"The only men she knew at home were loggers and mill workers like her father and brothers. Everyone just took for granted she'd marry one of them and settle down with a new television and a company trailer and a handful of kids. And if she was real lucky, she'd marry a man who didn't drink too much or beat her up too badly or gamble his paycheck away every weekend. And one smart enough to get himself killed outright in the mill instead of just maimed—that way she'd get a nice company pension instead of welfare.''

Dani shivered involuntarily. Jake glanced at her. "I was her ticket out. A college-educated rancher with money in my pocket, land of my own—I was her key to freedom. We were married two months later." He laughed bitterly. "Problem was, the only ranches she'd ever seen were on television. She moved in expecting barn dances and Sunday barbecues, weekend trips to Vancouver, camping under the stars, romantic trail rides—and found out that a real ranch is hard work and long hours."

Dani glanced at him and saw a muscle ripple in his jaw as though he had his teeth clenched. "She was bored and she was lonely, and she started drinking to make her days go by. At night, after I'd finished outside, I'd come in and she'd be waiting for me, wanting to go into town. It finally got so I'd just tell her to go if it would make her happy." The muscle in his jaw rippled, and he took a deep breath.

"At first it was only once or twice a week, but soon it was every night. I should have seen what was happening. Or maybe I did and just didn't want to admit it. I don't know. She'd go into the hotel lounge and have a few drinks. Men would come in, see her there as pretty as anything they'd ever set eyes on before, and they'd buy her a drink. Maybe two."

Dani knew what was coming. She put her hand out tentatively, touching his arm. "Jake..."

"I heard people talking, but I'd already guessed what was going on. I tried to talk to her, but she'd just laugh at me and tell me if I didn't give her the fun she wanted, she could find a hundred others who would. She loved being the center of things, having every man in the place watching her, wanting her."

He inhaled deeply. "It got so we weren't even talking, except to argue. I tried hiding the truck keys, but she'd coax one of the hired hands into taking her in, or walk out to the highway and hitch a ride. She didn't care if she got home or not. Hell, I can't count the number of nights I sat up, not knowing who to call, wondering if she was hurt or ill, or just in a motel room with some stranger." His mouth twisted in a humorless smile. "I was her husband, and half the time I didn't know where she was or who she was with!"

"Oh, Jake," Dani said, sighing, not knowing what else to say. Or maybe he didn't need her to say anything, she decided. Maybe he just needed someone to listen.

"When she got pregnant with Cassie, I thought it would all end. God, what a damn fool!" He laughed harshly again. "She was furious—blamed me for getting her pregnant deliberately, for ruining her life, her figure, her future. Ruining everything, period. For the first three months I was terrified to leave her alone in case she hurt either herself or the baby. Then, for a while, she seemed to settle down. She'd go for days without saying a word to me, but that was better than the yelling and shouting. And at least she was staying home at night and not drinking so heavily. For a little while I honestly thought . . ."

He let his words trail off, then after a moment or two shook his head. "Anyway, it didn't last. A month after Cassie was born, Sandra took the truck into town one afternoon and left the baby in the crib. I went after her and tried to bring her home, but she went crazy—screaming and shouting and throwing things. I guess I went a little crazy, too, but all I could see was Cassie lying in that crib, soaking wet and hungry, while Sandra sat in some bar. I wound up grabbing her and carrying her out, with her screaming and fighting like a wildcat and everyone in the bar applauding as though I'd finally done something any *real* man would have done months ago."

His eyes narrowed slightly. "When I got her home, I told her point-blank I wasn't taking any more. She could either get her act straightened out and stay—or get the hell out. And if she left, she was leaving alone. I wasn't letting her take Cassie. Believe it or not, I actually thought she'd decide to stay. But she didn't. A week later she was gone. I never found out where she went, and I never looked. I filed for divorce—it was never contested. I've never heard from her since.''

"My God," Dani whispered. "She left you with a month-old baby to raise."

"It was easier than you'd imagine. Sandra had refused to breast-feed, so we didn't have that to worry about. Buster and I took turns staying with Cassie. Some days I'd just stick her in one saddlebag and a bundle of diapers and formula bottles in the other and take her out with me." He laughed with real humor. "She loved it. No doubt that's why she's such a hellion on horseback now. She's probably the only kid whose rocking horse was real! She got so she'd sleep anywhere and through anything, and never seemed to mind eating at odd hours. If I was going out in the truck, I'd take her in her basket. I've sunk many a fence post with her lying beside me sound asleep.''

Dani had to laugh, sharing the joy he so obviously took in his daughter. "She takes after you a lot, I think. Strong, proud and as resilient as hell.''

He smiled faintly. "Funny, I've never told anyone about Sandra before. Not all of it.''

"It takes a long time to let it all go," she said quietly. "Especially the guilt. You tell yourself you could have prevented it, that if you'd tried harder or had paid more attention or had done more of this or less of that. I guess it's easier to take on the guilt than admit you made a mistake by choosing the wrong person in the first place.''

"That sounds like firsthand experience.''

It was Dani's turn to stare at the mountains. "It is. My own marriage broke up because I married the wrong man for the wrong reasons. And then I watched my parents split up three years ago.''

Jake gave a low whistle. "I think that's tougher than going through it yourself."

Dani managed a rough smile. "It's kind of like watching every childhood dream you ever had fall apart. Parents are *forever*! If they have feet of clay, what do you believe in?"

Jake nodded slowly. "Tell me about your client."

He was looking at the mountains again, his eyes narrowed and thoughtful, and Dani sighed inwardly. "Her name is Caroline Wainwright—you may have heard the name." She paused, but Jake shook his head. "Wainwright Industries is a heavyweight presence both here and overseas. Caroline's older sister, Marion, is the CEO. She's been running the business for over fifteen years, and she runs everything else in her life with the same no-nonsense efficiency—including her sister.

"Caroline is finishing up her graduate degree in medieval studies at the University of Toronto, and prefers staying at home with her books and dogs to playing social butterfly. She's twenty-nine, has never been married, is very pretty..." Dani shrugged. "All this information is in the portfolio I sent up—I'll give you a copy when we get back to the house."

"Why is her sister so anxious to get her married off?"

"Marion is on her third husband, and she considers Caroline's spinsterhood, as she delicately puts it, an oddity. Their parents died in a car accident years ago, and Marion has always taken care of Caroline. It's a role she can't seem to shake. She had a brush with cancer last year, and I think she's worried that if something happens to her, Caroline won't be able to manage on her own."

Dani smiled. "Personally, I doubt that. Caroline struck me as an eminently practical woman. But there's no arguing with Marion. Part of it is sincere sisterly concern and part is...well, just Marion. She likes an orderly universe. And she isn't the least bit shy about taking matters into her own hands if divine providence seems to be taking too long."

"And what does Caroline think about having her life run like this?"

Dani slipped him an amused look. "You're probably going to find this as hard to believe as I did at first, but she's completely agreeable to the idea. She'd like to be married, have children, a home...all the usual things, but is so shy that meeting men is difficult. And being a Wainwright makes it more difficult because there's always the chance of being taken in by a fortune hunter more interested in Daddy's millions than in Caroline herself. She's also apparently quite a romantic, always falling in love with every man she *does* meet. According to Marion, she's fallen for at least two gardeners and a chimney sweep, and I suspect Marion wants Caroline safely married just for her own peace of mind."

Jake gave a noncommittal grunt, still studying the horizon. Dani looked at him seriously. "I've spent quite a bit of time with her, Jake, and I like her very much. She's got a terrific sense of humor; she's extremely pretty—I already said that, didn't I?" She frowned. "Damn, this is like trying to describe the ultimate blind date!"

"So you believe it can work, do you? This arranged marriage idea?"

"I think an arranged marriage has as good if not a better chance of succeeding than one where two people are madly in love," she said quietly. "People get so caught up with being in love that they blind themselves to all the reasons why it can't work. Then one day they wake up and see all the things they refused to see before, and they get angry and resentful and people get hurt. At least this way you know exactly what you're getting into. It might not be very romantic, whatever that means, but it's practical."

"Is that what happened to you?" Jake stared at her thoughtfully, a small frown wedged between his brows.

"I fell in love with Darren when I was fifteen years old. We were classic childhood sweethearts, and it never occurred to me that we wouldn't be together for the rest of our lives. I never even dated anyone else, can you believe that?'' She smiled, then let it fade. ''I was nineteen when we got married. He was twenty-two. The first year was like magic.'' She looked up at Jake. ''Sometimes I try to remember what it was like, being that much in love. But I can't. It seems like a dream now.''

''What happened?''

''I woke up one morning and realized I was married to a chronic liar and an alcoholic.'' She said it bluntly, wanting to get it over with. ''He couldn't hold a job for more than a few weeks. I'd convinced myself he was a free spirit stifled by rules, but he was just irresponsible and lazy. When he was drinking, he was everyone's friend, full of dreams and plans that never got off the ground. When he was sober, he was moody and belligerent and would go for days without saying a word. The day I realized I preferred him drunk to sober was the day I left.'' She looked up at him evenly. ''That was the day I finally realized that love is like Santa Claus— a myth we all believe in until we grow up and see life as it really is.''

''And this marriage,'' he said carefully, ''it's . . . real?''

''Do you mean, will she sleep with you?'' she asked bluntly. It was a reasonable question, considering the circumstances, but for some reason it irritated her.

Jake's eyes narrowed. ''That's one way of putting it.''

''The marriage will be real, Mr. Montana,'' Dani said crisply. ''Caroline isn't naive. I'm hardly in the position to advise you of your marital arrangements, but I imagine she'll be expecting to sleep with you, in the fullest sense of the expression.''

He flushed slightly at her tone. ''There was something in the papers you sent Buster about a prenuptial agreement.''

''It simply states that you understand that when Caroline marries, she relinquishes all claim to the family money or business. She will retain her trust fund, of course, and she can do whatever she wishes with it. But if you divorce, you lose all claim to that, as well.''

"Cautious bunch, aren't they?"

Dani shrugged. "It's normal for families with holdings like the Wainwrights to protect their interests. Do you have a problem with that?"

"I don't need the Wainwrights' money."

Dani nodded. It was strange, but in the space of a few moments Jake had changed. Gone was the happy-go-lucky cowboy with the reckless grin whose lake-blue eyes had made her heart skip a beat every time they met hers. In his place was a tall, somber-eyed rancher, shrewd and matter-of-fact and a trifle cold. Suddenly she was the businesswoman again, he the client, and the only thing they had in common was a briefcase filled with contracts.

She took one last, regretful look at the mountains, then started walking to where Cherokee and the chestnut mare were grazing. Tinkerbell threw her head up and snorted in feigned alarm, then whickered a soft greeting.

Dani rubbed the mare's velvet nose, and she bumped her big head against Dani's chest, rubbery lips fumbling at the front of Dani's sweater. Cherokee came over to see what was happening and blew gustily down Dani's back. She slapped his neck, and the big horse rubbed his face on her shoulder, nipping harmlessly at her sleeve.

"I'm sorry."

Jake's quiet voice came from right behind her, and Dani stiffened slightly. She ran her hand down Tinkerbell's nose, not turning around. "For what?"

"I thought you'd be glad."

"I am," Dani said lightly. She combed the mare's tangled forelock with her fingers. "Once the papers are signed, I can go home."

"Is that what you want, Dani?" Two large, warm hands cupped her shoulders and Dani froze, hardly daring to breathe. He lowered his face slowly until his lips brushed the side of her throat. "Is that really what you want?"

"Of course." Dani's voice was so unsteady that she hardly recognized it. "Wh-why wouldn't I? Then I'm finished here."

"Are you?" he whispered. He started kissing her, tiny, biting little kisses that ran slowly down to her nape, then around the other side of her neck. "I know at least one good reason why you should stay, Dani. And so do you."

His mouth was hot and moist, and she could feel the silk of his tongue, the latent tension in his fingers as they tightened on her shoulders. She wanted to scream at him to stop this craziness, but she could no more have broken the magic spell of his touch than fly. Her heart was pounding now, and she felt dizzy and drugged and knew it was only a matter of time before her knees gave out.

"I want you."

He whispered the words so softly that she wondered if he'd said them, or if she'd simply imagined them, but knew as his mouth glided over her that it didn't matter. She was turning toward him even as he was pulling her around, and a moment later she was in his arms and his mouth was on hers.

He breached the barricade of her lips with one vital thrust of his tongue and kissed her with intoxicating urgency. He held nothing back, and Dani felt the last of her willpower dissolve as his mouth moved over hers hungrily, so explicit in its demand that she felt faint. His tongue brushed hers, and Dani groaned and pressed against him, half-wild from the feel of him.

Jake growled something, half lifting her, and Dani sank her fingers into his thick hair as his kiss deepened. She felt the strong thrust of his thigh between hers and she whimpered softly, her body aching for that intimate caress. He flexed his thigh gently, knowing exactly what she wanted, needed. He caught one of her hands in his and drew it slowly down.

Even expecting it, Dani had to catch her breath as he pressed her hand against himself. The touch of him, the soft catch in his voice when he groaned her name, was blatantly erotic. She sagged against him, and in the next instant they were kneeling. Then Jake lowered her gently to the ground. His hand was at her waist, tugging her sweater up roughly, and before she could catch her breath his mouth had settled over her breast.

Through silk, he tasted her. The nipple was already so sensitive that the touch of his tongue made her groan, and she arched her back, pressing his mouth against her. Her blouse and the thin lace of her bra were wet, and he suckled her gently, the friction of the thin material between them heightening the sensation until she could hardly stand it. He caught the tiny bud between his teeth and tugged gently, and Dani cried out, knowing she should be stopping him, that this was absolute madness.

But it was even greater madness to pretend she didn't want what they were doing to continue as badly as he did. It was pointless to wonder why, pointless to remind herself that she didn't do things like make love with perfect strangers in mountain meadows. All she knew was that she wanted to be naked in his arms, to have those strong hands touch her in ways no man had ever touched her before, to have him so deeply inside her she'd never be entirely free of him.

The click of a horseshoe beside her ear made her open her eyes and she found herself looking into Cherokee's liquid brown eye. He snorted and blew gently in her face, and she was turning her head away when a movement far down the hillside caught her eye. She frowned, only half aware that Jake had tugged her shirt out of the waistband of her slacks and was kissing her bare stomach.

"Jake." Her fingers tightened involuntarily in his hair. "Jake, someone's coming!"

Jake only half heard her. The skin on her abdomen was like satin, and he ran his tongue across it slowly.

"Cassie . . . I think it's Cassie."

Cherokee gave a loud whinny, and Jake groaned. He turned his head to see what Dani was looking at. It was

Cassie all right, riding her fat little paint at a flat-out gallop. She was lying against his withers, her hair streaming out behind her like a banner. Apache was straining hard, and as he came charging up to the hillside, Jake could see the sweat runneling down his chest, the streamers of foam along his muzzle and neck.

He was on his feet with an oath, his stomach twisting into a hard knot. Something was wrong. As fearless and madcap a rider as Cassie was, she knew better than to abuse a horse like that. She loved her pony too much to endanger him without good reason.

"Jake, what is it?" Dani was on her feet a second later, tucking her shirt into her slacks and adjusting her sweater.

"Trouble." He shaded his eyes with his hand and watched as Cassie neared. Apache cleared the crest of the hill and galloped straight at them.

"Daddy! Daddy, you've gotta come quick! It's Gran'pa!" Cassie pulled the pony up too hard, and he reared with a squeal.

Jake grabbed the halter and dragged the horse down, reaching out to swing Cassie off the animal's back. Apache stopped fighting and stood trembling from ear to fetlock, sides heaving like a bellows under the lather of sweat.

Cassie was trembling almost as badly. "It's Gran'pa! He fell down, and his leg's broke real bad. Cochise an' Jesse took him to the hospital, an' Jesse told me to find you and—" The rest was lost as she suddenly burst into tears and catapulted herself into Jake's arms.

Dani's eyes met his across Cassie's shoulder. Her face was pale. "Go," she said evenly, reaching to take Cassie from him. "I'll take Cassie home and stay with her. If—" She swallowed. "If it's as bad as it sounds, they might want you to stay at the hospital."

"But your plane..."

"Forget the plane!" She gently removed Cassie's arms from around his neck and took the weeping child into her own arms, cradling her. "There's always another plane. Just get going!"

He hesitated, then turned and snatched up Cherokee's reins, pulling the horse around. "I'll call you from the hospital."

She nodded, then hugged Cassie as Jake leaned down and kissed her fiercely on the mouth. He squeezed her shoulder to reassure her, then turned and mounted. Cherokee shook his head and danced sideways, infected with the tension he sensed. Jake wheeled him around and touched him with his boot heels, feeling the horse's powerful haunches bunch. Then Cherokee was plunging down the hillside.

He'd been here before. Jake leaned heavily against the split-log mantel of the fireplace and stared down into the crackling flames, aching with exhaustion and worry. He'd stood right here two years ago, wondering if his grandfather was ever going to walk again. It sometimes seemed as though the harder he tried to hold the tattered strands of his life together, the more determined they were to slip from his grasp.

A log snapped, sending up a shower of hissing sparks, and Jake blinked, trying to shake himself free of his black mood. They'd made it the last time; they'd make it this time, too.

He heard quiet footsteps across the hardwood floor, and a moment later Dani appeared beside him. She looked as exhausted as he felt. Her face was drawn and the delicate skin under her eyes looked bruised. Her condition shocked him slightly, and he wondered why he hadn't noticed it before, then immediately chided himself for allowing the indulgence of self-pity while forgetting that Dani had been here alone with Cassie all day and half the night.

He managed a weak smile and reached out to take her hand. "How are you doing?"

"I'm okay." She smiled up at him wearily. "The question is, how are you? You look like hell, to be blunt."

Jake rubbed his chin, fingers rasping against an eighteen-hour growth of beard. He smiled faintly. "I'll live. How's Cass?"

"Sound asleep, finally. She's been running on empty for hours. I had to swear a solemn oath not to leave without saying goodbye—and to wake her up if we heard anything about Buster."

"I checked with the hospital again a few minutes ago, and he's doing fine. He was out of the anesthesia when I left, but they've sedated him again and he's sleeping comfortably."

"Are you going back?"

Jake frowned, rubbing his bristly cheek. "I'd intended to. I just came home to clean up a bit and spend some time with Cass. But the doctor said there wasn't much point—that he'll sleep until late morning. And they'll call if his condition changes."

Dani put her hand on his shoulder and gently kneaded the taut muscles. "Jake, why don't you have a hot shower while I scrounge up something to eat? There's some leftover chicken—I can make you a sandwich and heat up some soup. You haven't had anything but vending machine coffee all day and you're dead on your feet."

Jake managed a grin. "You take such good care of me, honey."

"Don't push your luck, cowboy."

Jake let the grin fade, too bone-tired even to continue the teasing. "I'm glad you're here, Dani," he said quietly. "Knowing Cass was safe with you was a real load off my mind today. If you hadn't been here, I'd have had to take her with me—and a hospital's no place for a kid. I think that's what scared her so badly last time we took Buster in. Jesse and Cochise do their best, but..." He shrugged and looked down into the flames. Then he gave Dani a sidelong glance. "But that's not the only reason."

"Jake..." She held her hands out as though to stop him.

"Dani," he said quietly, "what happened out there this morning—"

"I don't want to talk about it."

"I do." He reached out and tipped her chin up with his fingers, forcing her to look at him. "Dani, I didn't plan what happened. You'd made it plain enough you weren't interested last night, and I'm not the kind of man who figures 'no' is just a challenge to try harder." He had no idea why he was telling her this, but for some reason it seemed important.

"I know that." She looked away again. "I'm being paid to know you better than you do, remember?"

"I don't even know how it happened," he said softly. "One minute we were talking about arranged marriages, and the next you were in my arms and everything just went a little crazy."

Dani drew in a deep breath and looked up at him. "Jake, I think the best idea for all concerned is for us to just forget it ever happened. We'll put it down to a...a momentary lapse."

"That was no momentary lapse," Jake growled. "And you—"

"Jake, as long as you're considering marrying Caroline Wainwright, you and I are business associates." She lifted her chin with determination. "I don't socialize with the people I do business with, and anything that's happened between us is...well, it's just better forgotten, that's all."

Her expressive eyes were shuttered, cool. It was as though there was suddenly a conference table between them, as though she'd already slipped out of the casual slacks and sweater and was back in her designer-label power suit.

Jake snorted. "It's a little late to be hauling up the drawbridges, buttercup. That flint-eyed, lady-executive routine might work in Toronto, but it's going to take a hell of a lot more to make me forget this morning. I was the guy up there on that hillside with you, remember? I was the guy who was—"

"Jake, please!" She clenched her fists, her voice desperate. "I know I'm handling this badly, but I've never had anything like this happen to me before! I don't just fall into a man's arms at eight in the morning and practically beg him to make love to me!'' She looked so upset that Jake nearly had to laugh. ''But I do know this is a job and you're my client and I've broken all the rules and—''

''Not broken,'' Jake said with a reassuring grin. ''You've maybe *bent* a couple, but they're still all in one piece.''

To his relief, Dani took his teasing in stride and visibly relaxed. ''I'm sorry. I don't usually react like *that*, either.''

''It's been a hell of a day,'' Jake said quietly. ''I don't think either of us is reacting very normally. What do you say to calling it a draw?''

''Yeah.'' She nodded, finally smiling at him. ''That would be nice.''

''I'm going to have that shower.'' He moved away from the mantel. ''And that sandwich sounded great.''

''Jake?''

Her voice stopped him, and he glanced around.

''What happened this morning...I'm not going to be able to forget it, either. But I shouldn't have *let* it happen. Not with you, not under the circumstances. I shouldn't have let you think...'' She shrugged and looked down uncomfortably. ''I've made it awkward for both of us, and I'm sorry.''

''I'm not,'' Jake said quietly. ''Meeting you has been the highlight of the past two years. Everything's going to be downhill from here.'' He turned away and walked out the door.

It was strange, Dani mused as she watched Jake walk away, how two people could communicate so perfectly without ever speaking a word. She and Darren had talked endlessly during their marriage without saying a thing, yet Jake could tell her everything she needed to know in one glance.

Which wasn't, when she thought about it, really strange at all. She sighed and turned back to the fire, massaging the muscles in her neck with both hands. In fact, the only thing surprising about the chemistry that had sprung up between Jake and her was that it *had* surprised her.

She'd thought about it a lot that afternoon. Alone with Cassie, worried and anxious and waiting for Jake to phone, there had been little else to do. And she had slowly started to understand.

She'd written the ad that had started the ball rolling in her search for the Ideal Man. She'd chosen the possible candidates, had sorted through all the responses. She'd had constant input from Caroline, but basically it had been *her* instincts that had gone into the choosing.

Was it any surprise then that the Ideal Man she'd finally discovered was her *own* Ideal Man as well as Caroline's? If Jake Montana *hadn't* ignited some pretty serious sparks, she should have taken it as a sign that something was wrong.

Figuring it out had made her feel better. Knowing that she was simply reacting to Jake as she should be reacting meant all those months of hard work had paid off. What it also meant, of course, was that she was going to have to be scrupulous about keeping her relationship with Jake strictly business. Her fee, after all, was for finding a suitable husband for Caroline, not for sampling the merchandise.

Dani smiled to herself. Poor Jake! He was even more confused about what was going on than she was. He didn't understand that he was just a victim of his own success!

When Jake came into the kitchen nearly twenty minutes later, he looked almost human again. He still looked tired, but he'd shaved and changed into fresh clothes. His hair was still wet from the shower. It glittered under the harsh ceiling light, and although he'd tried to comb it down, it was already drying into a seductive nest of tangled curls that displayed a dozen shades of gold, from sun-bleached silver-white, to brown sugar. His bronzed cheeks were smooth and slightly damp, and when he walked by her, Dani caught the clean, heathery scent of soap and shampoo.

He sat at the table where she'd set a place for him without saying a thing, frowning faintly as he toyed with the spoon. She put the steaming bowl of chowder in front of him, and he just stared into it.

"Corn." Dani smiled when he blinked and looked up slowly. "It's corn chowder."

He looked down at it as though seeing it for the first time. Then he put the spoon down very carefully. "I want you to stay, Dani. Here, I mean. On Silvercreek."

Six

Dani simply stared at him.

"Dani, I can't do it alone—not with Buster in the hospital. Not run Silvercreek and take care of Cassie, too."

"Jake, you can't be serious. I've got a job to go back to. In fact, I'm supposed to be doing my job right now, not making you sandwiches and soup. If I was half the corporate executive I'm supposed to be, I'd have my contract on the table showing you where to sign so I could leave first thing in the morning. I can't possibly—"

"Damn it, Dani, they'll take Cass away!" He leaned forward, his gaze fierce. "This is all the excuse that social services woman needs to put Cass in a foster home."

"But—"

"Time, Dani, that's all I need. Just some time." He reached out, caught her hands and pulled her gently toward him. "Dani, if you've learned anything about me these past couple of days, you should know I don't find it easy to ask for help. But damn it, I can't lose Cassie! Just stay long enough for me to find a good housekeeper. That's all I'm asking."

Staring down into those dark eyes, Dani could feel panic starting to rise. She couldn't stay! She didn't dare....

"A week at the outside, Dani. That's all I'm asking," Jake said softly.

She wheeled away and stood by the sink, trying to get her racing thoughts in order.

"Please, Dani." His voice was a coaxing purr of sound, coming from right behind her. Even expecting his touch, she started when his hands settled on her shoulders. "Stay, Dani, just until everything gets sorted out. Stay with me...."

Dani's fingers were aching where she gripped the edge of the counter. Her chest felt so tight that she could barely breathe, and she was almost screaming with the tension, knowing he was going to kiss her, knowing if he did she was going to be all but helpless to stop him. "On one condition," she finally managed to get out.

"Name it." His breath curled around the nape of her neck.

"That *this*—" she stepped away from him, praying her legs would hold up "—ends here and now." She turned to look up at him, feeling her heart do one of those weird little tumbles as his eyes captured hers. "We ... we can't keep doing this, Jake."

"Doing what, buttercup?" There may have been a hint of laughter around his mouth.

"Jake," she said warningly, "listen to me! As long as you're considering marrying Caroline Wainwright, you're off-limits as far as I'm concerned. And the *only* way I'll agree to stay here with you even another hour is if you swear to me that this will stop. What we're feeling isn't real. It's a combination of sexual attraction, stress, opportunity, maybe a bit of loneliness, a bit of curiosity. And the greatest aphrodisiac of all—no strings."

He winced, then laughed. "God, you can be brutal!"

"But I'm right." Dani smiled. "Come on, Jake, admit it. You find me attractive because I'm not a threat. I'm not going to get silly after a few days and expect you to marry me. I'm a practical woman. I'm not about to start demanding things you can't give, then go off slamming doors because I don't get them. You know that I'll thank you very much for the memories and head back to Toronto, and you'll never hear from me again."

He was still looking at her, almost wistfully now. "You almost make me wish it wasn't true, buttercup. You almost make me wish..." He let the thought trail off, then leaned down, brushing his lips lightly across hers. "You win. I'll consider myself a next-to-married man and behave myself. Now will you stay?"

Dani looked at him closely, suspicious of how easily he'd capitulated. It was sheer insanity, even considering staying....

"For Cassie's sake, if not mine," he urged her gently. "And Buster's. He won't be rampaging to get out of the hospital before he's properly healed if he knows you're here with Cass and that social services woman can't—"

"Enough! My God, of all the manipulative, conniving—"

"Does that mean you'll stay?"

"For Cassie's sake," she told him. "And for Buster. And I'll give you a week. Five days, Montana. If you don't have someone up here by then, you're on your own."

He at least had the decency to wipe the grin off his mouth.

"Well, I don't mind telling you," Buster said with a decisive nod of his head, "that it's a load off my mind! I've been lying here worrying about how Jake was going to handle Silvercreek and Cassie all by himself. I was all set to grab my clothes and hightail it out of here when they hog-tied me to *this* contraption." He nodded toward his right leg, which was suspended above the bed in a complicated array of slings and pulleys. "Some fancy new gadget they're trying out," he grumbled. "I'll tell you, these people love nothing better than gettin' a helpless old man in here to poke and prod!"

Dani swallowed a smile, thinking that she'd rarely met anyone less helpless than Buster Greaves. When she, Jake and Cassie had come in, they'd heard his bellowing all the way down by the elevators. They'd found him holding court with a doctor and a collection of young interns, all of them standing silent and wide-eyed as Buster told them in colorful, straightforward English what he thought of the entire medical community and its suspect practices.

"When are you comin' home, Gran'pa?" Cassie leaned across the edge of the bed, her face screwed up with a worried frown as she eyed the intravenous bottles and tubing.

Buster stroked her hair. "Not too long, honey. Them dang doctors want to make sure their fancy needlework holds together before they turn me loose, that's all."

"Aside from all the indignities," Dani said with a laugh, "how are they treating you?"

"Like some damn old cripple," he growled. "Can't do this, can't do that. You see that bunch that was in here? They weren't even *real* doctors. Not one of 'em old enough to shave, even if half of 'em weren't women. 'Bringing 'em around for geriatric experience,' the doctor heading 'em up said." Buster let loose a gargantuan snort. "'Geriatric experience!' I was ready to geriatric the lot of 'em, I'll tell you."

"Your doctor says you came through surgery like a twenty-year-old," Dani said. "He said if everything continues as well as it's been going so far, you'll be home by the end of the month." *But not on your feet,* she added silently, knowing Buster was thinking the same thing. It was going to take weeks for the shattered bones to mend, followed by months of arduous, painful therapy to get him even partially mobile.

"Can't be too soon for me," Buster muttered darkly.

"Why don't you just take advantage of it?" Jake offered. "Lie back and let people wait on you like royalty. Dani and I can hold things together until you get back."

Buster gave him a ferocious scowl. "If it was you in here strung up like a side of beef with your bare backside flapping outta your nightie, you wouldn't be quite so easygoin'!"

Cassie gave a gasp of delighted laughter and looked up at her father. Jake smiled down at her and dropped his Stetson onto her head. She gave a muffled squeak, momentarily blinded as it covered her eyes, then pushed it back far enough to peer out from under the brim.

"I'm going to sign the agreement," Jake said quietly.

"What agreement?" Buster gave him a sharp look.

"Dani's agreement."

"You two gettin' married?"

"Not Dani, for—!" Jake caught himself, then took a deep breath. "Her client. You were the one writing back and forth—you should know more about this Caroline than I do!"

"Oh." Buster shot Dani a speculative look. "Why don't you marry him yourself? Seems a shame, wastin' him like that. A woman could do a damn sight worse."

"I'm sure she could," Dani said with a quiet laugh, avoiding Jake's eyes. "But I'm not in the market for a husband, remember?"

Buster grunted and looked up at Jake. "You got a chance to get yourself one hell of a good woman here, if you play your cards right. Do your courtin' like I taught you, and you could change her mind."

"Buster!" Dani had to laugh at him, knowing she should be furious at the old man's meddling but unable to find even the tiniest bit of resentment. "I'm going to recommend that ManHunters Incorporated hire you as their resident matchmaker. You've obviously got the persistence it takes!"

"Just trying to get the best for my grandson, that's all," he protested with a chuckle. He suddenly looked at something over Dani's head and broke into a beaming smile.

Dani glanced behind her just as the woman came into the room. She was smartly dressed and attractive, perhaps in her late fifties, with a serene face and calm blue eyes. She smiled at Jake and Buster, and then at Cassie, her expression warming.

"Hi, Ms. Wilson!" Cassie tipped her head well back, peering out from under the brim of Jake's hat like a bright-eyed mouse. "Are you here to visit Gran'pa?"

"Hi, yourself! I heard your great-grandfather was in here and thought he might need some cheering up." She leaned over and gave Buster a light kiss on the cheek. "And hi to you, too."

"Daddy, Ms. Wilson just—*mmph*!"

Dani looked at Cassie and found her encompassed in her father's arms, one of his large hands clamped firmly across her mouth. He squatted on his heels and whispered something into her ear, and Dani watched as her eyes widened and she nodded vigorously. Jake took his hand away, and Cassie leaned her elbows on the side of the bed again, gazing at Beth Wilson wonderingly. Dani raised an inquiring eyebrow at Jake, but he just smiled.

"And you've got to be the famous Dani Ross." Beth smiled warmly at her. "Your ears must have been burning the night before last. All Cassie and Buster could talk about was the new woman in Jake's life."

"I, umm, how do you do?" Slightly nonplussed, Dani smiled. "Yours were probably burning for much the same reason. Jake was telling me all about the work you're doing with the local kids. And I'm fascinated with the play."

"Well, it turned into more work than I'd anticipated, but isn't that always the way?" She laughed merrily. "Maybe you'll help me next year. I could certainly use someone with your talents in costuming!"

"I wish I could, but I'm going back to Toronto soon."

"Oh, I'm sorry. I thought you and Jake . . . that is, I was led to believe . . ." Beth looked at Jake, then at Dani again. "I mean, I thought Buster said . . . oh, my!"

She looked so genuinely distressed that Dani had to laugh. "Don't apologize! I get confused whenever I'm around this bunch, too. But I'm just up here for a brief visit. I'm a . . . friend of the family." *Which wasn't quite a lie,* Dani told herself.

"A very *close* friend," Jake put in with a smile, giving Dani an outrageous wink. His large, warm hand settled over her thigh as he pushed himself to his feet.

"I think," Dani said firmly, "that it's time we left."

"Ah, do we gotta go, Daddy?" Cassie gazed up at Jake.

"'Have to,' half-pint, not 'gotta.'" Jake reached down and rescued his hat, settling it over his own head. "And, yes, we do. We'll come back tomorrow."

Cassie wrinkled her nose, leaned over and gave Buster a huge hug. "Bye, Gran'pa. I wish you could come home with us."

"I do, too, punkin." Buster hugged her tightly, then kissed her cheek. "Now I want you to mind Dani, hear me? When she tells you to do somethin', you jump to it—understand me?"

Cassie gave a subdued nod. "Yes, Gran'pa. I promise." She slid off the bed and reached up for the reassurance of her father's hand, and Jake, with a smile, picked her up and tossed her over his shoulder. Cassie gave a squeal of sheer delight, her unhappiness at leaving Buster momentarily forgotten, and Dani laughed as the two of them headed for the door.

Dani started to turn away, then impulsively bent to plant a kiss on Buster's cheek. "You take care of yourself—and don't get fresh with the nurses!"

He wrapped his hands around hers. "Take good care of my grandson while I'm in here, okay?"

"Promise." She squeezed the gnarled fingers. "Don't worry about either of them."

"You're a good woman, Dani Ross," he murmured, his eyes holding hers. "You should think about what I was saying. About you marryin' Jake, that is. He'd make you happy—and I know you make him happy!"

Dani felt herself blush. "You really are a persistent old devil!" She walked around the end of the bed toward the door and smiled at Beth. "It's nice to have met you. Good luck with opening night!"

"You *are* going to be able to come, aren't you?" Beth asked.

"Well, I don't know if—"

"Oh, please try!" Beth smiled engagingly. "It's just next week. Surely you'll still be here. I've already talked to the doctors about smuggling Buster out in a wheelchair for a couple of hours so he can see it. But it would be really special for her if you were there, too." She smiled down at Buster, then looked at Dani again, more seriously now.

"Jake and Buster do a wonderful job, but Cassie misses out not having a mother. The other children tease her about it sometimes, and although she pretends it doesn't bother her, I know it does. Now please don't take this the wrong way—I know you're not . . . well, trying to be a mother to Cassie or anything—but having you there with Jake and Buster would really make her evening one to remember." She laughed suddenly, looking embarrassed. "Sometimes I can't believe how pushy I can get! I hope you'll forgive me."

"Hey, Dani, Daddy's buyin' ice cream, so you'd better hurry up!" Cassie's voice floated by the door, fading with distance.

Dani laughed. "I'd better go. I promise I'll try my best, Beth. And, Buster, I'll see you tomorrow!"

"So." Jake poured himself a large mug of steaming hot coffee and carried it over to the kitchen table. "What's your assessment of the situation—is she sweet on him or not?"

Dani glanced up from the potato she was peeling. "Would it bother you if they *were* serious?"

"Not particularly. It would mean some changes around here, but I figure Buster deserves a bit of happiness. His life hasn't been all roses."

"He raised you more or less by himself, didn't he?"

"My mother wasn't even sixteen when she had me," Jake said quietly. "Did Buster ever tell you how I got my name?" When Dani shook her head, Jake smiled faintly and turned the coffee mug in his hands. "I was christened 'Jake' because my mother didn't know how to spell 'Jack' on the forms, and 'Montana' because the only thing she knew about my father was that he was from that state."

The smile turned bitter. "He was a bronc rider in town for the weekend, up from the States riding the rodeo circuit. I doubt she saw him more than the once. For years I hung around every rodeo that hit the Cariboo, hoping to find a man called Montana Jack, but I never did." He laughed ruefully and looked at Dani. "Probably a good thing. I doubt he'd have appreciated some skinny kid coming up and calling him Daddy."

"There's a country and western ballad in there somewhere." Dani smiled, picked up her mug of coffee and walked across to the table. "And your mother? Buster wasn't very clear on what happened to her, just that he wound up raising you."

Jake stared into his coffee. "I was too young to remember the details. Most of what I know is what Buster told me. My grandmother died not long after I was born, and I guess things weren't great between my mother and Buster." He laughed softly. "Hell, you know him. From what he says, she was just like him—stubborn, proud, hardheaded. One day when I was about five she couldn't take it any longer and she walked out. She never came back."

"Oh, Jake," Dani said, sighing. "Did you ever hear from her?"

"Buster got a letter a couple of years later from Los Angeles. She had a bit part in some movie, and when she got enough money together she was going to send for me. But, of course, she didn't. The L.A. police notified us six months later that she'd been killed in a car accident. I don't think Buster ever entirely forgave himself. He put a lot of extra care into raising me to make it up to her.''

Dani put her hand on his shoulder and rubbed the knotted muscles at the back of his neck. ''Family are sure hard on each other, aren't they?''

He leaned back, sighing with pleasure, his eyes closed. ''You sound like you come from pretty normal stock.''

Dani laughed. ''Yeah, if you can call anyone normal. My dad's a farmer and grass-roots political activist who's always getting mad at some injustice and running for local office. He gets in now and again, too. My mother is into environmental issues and is quite proud of the night she spent in jail after picketing a local fertilizer plant.''

''You said they broke up a few years ago,'' he said gently.

Dani didn't realize she'd clenched her hands until Jake flinched slightly. She relaxed her fingers, concentrating on massaging his taut muscles. ''My three older brothers and my sister all took it in stride. They said they'd seen it coming for years. It hit Kevin, my younger brother, and me right out of the blue. I'd had no idea anything was wrong. They never argued, never seemed even to disagree…'' She thought about that for a moment. ''Maybe that was the biggest clue right there. Mom waited until Kev was in college and more or less on his own, then she packed up and left. Just like that.''

''Is your dad still on the farm?''

''Oh, yes. He loves the land too much to ever quit farming. Mom moved into her own apartment in Regina and is working in an arts and crafts shop. I hardly recognize her. She's lost weight and a lot of gray, has a new hairstyle and wardrobe. And she's happy. I have to admit that.'' She sighed. ''It's just…oh, I don't know. I always figured they'd be together forever, and when they divorced it was like the foundations of my world collapsed. Suddenly there wasn't *anything* I could count on anymore. Nothing I could trust.

It's like finding out that the people you believed in the most have been lying to you all along.''

"You sound close to your brothers and sister."

Dani had to laugh. "On and off. Living in a big family is like the world itself—there are always small wars springing up here and there, alliances being formed and broken, territories invaded, treaties negotiated. But it's better now that we're all grown. We've got...let's see. Two farmers, one dentist, one lawyer and a chemical engineer.''

"And you."

"And me."

"Headhunter and marriage broker."

"Headhunter. As soon as this job's over, I'm out of the marriage-broker business for keeps.''

"Seems to me you're pretty good at it." He opened his eyes and leaned his head back to look up at her. "You found me.''

They looked at each other for a moment, then Dani resumed massaging his neck, digging her fingers into the solid muscle forcefully. "For another woman."

The laughter vanished from Jake's eyes, and he straightened up and looked down at the papers scattered across the table. "True."

It took Dani a moment to realize they were the ones she had given him last night. The folder containing Caroline's biography was sitting to one side, and Jake was perusing the actual contract itself. She withdrew her hands from him slowly, then walked around the table and sat down.

He was frowning thoughtfully. "What exactly am I signing?''

"Just a statement that you know I'm here representing Caroline, that you're agreeable to marrying her and that you allow me to act on your behalf when I go back to meet with the Wainwrights.''

"Sign it, and I'm almost married."

"Almost." Dani frowned. Why did she feel so depressed? She'd done everything she'd set out to do six months ago. So why did she get this ache in her stomach every time she thought of Jake and Caroline together? "Think of it as an engagement, if you like."

After a long silence, he looked up at her. "I guess this is it."

"Second thoughts?"

He smiled faintly. "I need a wife and she wants a husband. Pretty simple when you think about it."

"Yeah." Dani's frown deepened.

"Are you?"

"Am I what?"

Jake gave her a slashing, rakehell grin. "Having second thoughts? About marrying me yourself?"

"You've been talking to Buster again, haven't you?"

But Jake just grinned. "He could be onto something. Seems to me we're two of a kind, you and me."

"Except for the fact that I'm not even remotely interested in getting married again." She said it much too sharply, making Jake look at her. Ignoring him, she got up quickly and carried her mug over to the stove.

"Last chance, buttercup," Jake said softly. "In another minute it'll be too late."

"Just sign the damn papers." Dani's hand ached where she gripped her mug too tightly. She poured herself more coffee, then turned and walked very calmly back to the table.

Jake was staring at the papers, pen in hand. Then, with a release of breath that could have been a sigh, he lowered the pen to the dotted line.

In the end Dani couldn't watch. She turned her head and stared out the window over the sink, watching a puff of cloud drift lazily across the sky. Feeling a surge of hopelessness so strong it took her breath away, she turned back to Jake. "Finished?"

Jake's face took on an odd expression she couldn't decipher, then he wordlessly held the sheaf of papers out. She took them and smiled with forced cheerfulness. "The final decision is Caroline's, of course," she said, "but I think it's safe to say she'll follow my recommendation. I'll call her right away." She was talking too quickly, her voice high and brittle, and Dani forced herself to stop. Her mouth ached with the strain of smiling, but she didn't dare let the smile slip, terrified of what might happen if it did.

Watching her, Jake found himself wondering why he felt such despair. No one had forced him to sign the agreement. Yet he was already regretting it. There was a part of him that said it made sense, but there was another part of him that wanted . . . what? He asked himself the question as he had a thousand times over the past couple of days, watching Dani as she read over the document. Her eyes seemed brighter than normal and she looked a little pale. Tired, probably. The strain of Buster's accident had taken a lot out of her, too.

He rubbed his forehead, trying to ease the nagging ache that had been there most of the day. He was tired, too. He'd been up and down a half-dozen times after he finally got to bed last night, either too hot or too cold, wanting the window closed, then open again. He'd wandered upstairs twice to check on Cassie for absolutely no reason.

He found himself watching Dani again. It was unnerving how easily she'd fit into his life. He'd always thought it would be difficult, getting used to having a woman around again. Yet Dani fitted here as though she belonged, as though he'd been holding a spot open for her all these years, knowing she'd come.

The house seemed filled with her. Last night, wandering around in the dark, he kept finding her things—a sweater tossed carelessly over the arm of a chair, a pair of earrings on the kitchen counter, a cup by the sink with her lipstick on it. And the dark rooms had been filled with her scent, tantalizing pockets of perfume in the still air that had made his breath catch every time he'd encountered one.

God, he was going to miss her when she left.

She looked up just then. Their eyes met, and time seemed to stop for that moment. Then Dani looked away abruptly, suddenly becoming very businesslike as she gathered the papers together. She got to her feet, and before he even realized what he was doing, Jake stood up and caught her by the arm, turning her toward him.

She stared up at him, then gave a half sob and stepped into his arms. Jake wrapped his arms around her and held her against him, his face buried in her hair. He could feel the warmth of her breath on his throat, the soft thrust of her breasts, her long thighs against his.

She fitted into the contours of his body as perfectly as she had into his life. There was no part of her that wasn't perfectly matched to him, and he hugged her fiercely, wanting to say so much yet not knowing the words. How could he say he loved her and wanted her always when he didn't even know what love was? How could he tell her she made him feel like no woman ever had, that he couldn't imagine spending another day of his life without her when he'd already signed the papers promising himself to another?

"Oh, Jake." She slipped her arms around him, holding him tightly. "We shouldn't, we promised ...!"

"I know." He held her even tighter, drinking in her warm, female scent like a thirsty man takes in the water he so desperately needs. "I know," he whispered. "But all the way back from the hospital in the truck you were sitting so close, and all I could think about was holding you."

"Jake, this is crazy!"

She lifted her face, and her mouth was under his, there for the taking. And take it he did, drowning in her, feeling her tremble as he drew her tongue into his mouth. Quickly he was fully aroused, his body shouting its need so vibrantly he realized he'd been waiting for this all day.

It was insane, kissing her like this here, now. Cassie would be slamming through the door any minute, then Cochise and Jesse, all ravenous as wolves. Yet he couldn't let her go if his life depended on it. He kissed her even more deeply and urgently, then pressed her against the counter and slid his leg between hers until he felt her give a little start as he moved against the softness between her legs. Thigh muscles tightening fiercely, she arched against him, her head falling back under the assault of his mouth.

Behind them someone cleared a throat.

Dani gave a convulsive gasp and clutched Jake's shoulders, eyes flying wide open. Jake reluctantly removed his mouth from hers and slowly let her slip out of his embrace, refusing to give their audience the satisfaction of completely ruining what had been a very enjoyable kiss. It was a little late to pretend they weren't doing what was obvious, and he saw damn little reason to hurry because someone had lousy timing.

Then there was another sound of a throat being cleared, this one louder than the first. Jake swore softly and wheeled around. "Damn it to hell, couldn't—*you*!"

The woman smiled. "I knocked, but you didn't hear me."

"I was busy."

"Yes, so I...noticed." Her pale brown eyes took in Dani's disheveled appearance.

Dani felt herself blush under the woman's cold appraisal, infuriated at being made to feel so vulnerable by someone she didn't even know. The woman was tall and slender, with narrow, foxlike features. Her gaze swept around the room, and Dani imagined she could hear the whir of the woman's brain as she cataloged, assessed and filed everything she saw.

There was something decidedly calculating in that look, and when it settled on her again, Dani bristled. "I don't think," she said in her most businesslike tone, "that we've met."

Before she could answer, Jake said, "Claudia Schefer, Department of Social Services."

Dani felt her blood run cold. She held the woman's stare steadily, refusing to be intimidated. "I wasn't aware that it was departmental policy for employees to enter a private residence uninvited." Her voice held all the authority she could muster, and even Jake looked at her in surprise.

Claudia's face turned an unattractive shade of pink. "Mr. Montana's truck is outside and the door was open. When no one answered my knock..." She shrugged, dismissing Dani's statement, then turned toward Jake, dismissing Dani as casually. "I heard your grandfather is in the hospital. How is he?"

"You mean you haven't checked?" Jake's eyes were cold.

Claudia's eyes turned even cooler. "I was told he won't be home for two to three weeks, and when he does come home, he'll be confined to bed or a wheelchair for weeks. Maybe months. They added that it was highly unlikely Mr. Greaves will ever walk again unaided."

Jake shrugged casually. "His doctors talk to me, too, Miss Schefer. You didn't have to come all the way out here to tell me something I already know."

The woman smiled a cold "I've got you where I want you now" smile that made Dani shiver. Obviously the woman's feud with Jake ran much deeper than simple departmental policy or concern for Cassie. Whatever had transpired between them in the past had cut right to the bone; Claudia Schefer was definitely out for blood.

"Is there something we can do for you?" she asked briskly.

They stared at each other for a long moment. Claudia's eyes narrowed, and Dani knew she was being sized up just as she was sizing up the other woman. She could almost feel the battle lines being drawn. And in that instant she understood perfectly. This didn't have anything to do with Cassie; it was about power.

Claudia had tried to bully Jake as she bullied everyone, but he'd stood up to her. And Claudia wasn't the type of woman who could accept defiance. It was a vendetta with her now. She wanted Jake brought down and brought down hard, and she was prepared to do everything necessary to get her way.

"May I ask who—?"

Claudia's question was cut short as the door flew open and Cassie hurtled into the room. She wore an Indian warbonnet made out of what looked like one of Jake's ties and a few dozen goose feathers. The only other thing she was wearing was a man's shirt, belted at the waist, the long tails flapping around her mud-spattered calves. She'd stuck a sheath knife into her belt—a very large, very real sheath knife, Dani noticed with a sinking heart, knowing that Claudia hadn't missed it, either—and was carrying a willow-branch bow and a fistful of sticks with feathers glued to them. Streaks of red poster paint decorated her dirty face, and she looked, Dani thought with wry amusement, every inch the little Indian warrior she was trying to imitate.

"Well, hello, Cassie." Claudia bent down to smile at the small girl. "How are you today?"

The headdress had slipped, and Cassie was obviously having trouble seeing. She had to tip her head back so that she could peer out from under the band at Claudia. "I'm okay," she whispered, pushing the headdress back. She seemed smaller somehow, defenseless, and Dani could see the sudden anxiety on her face, the way her eyes darted between Jake and Claudia.

"It's nearly time for supper, Cass," Dani said with a reassuring smile. "And I don't want you to take this personally or anything, but those hands look pretty dirty. Face, too."

Cassie nodded warily, walking well around Claudia as though around a viper pit. "I'm not going anywhere with you," she said in a clear voice. "You can't make me go."

"Nobody's taking you anywhere," Jake growled, slipping his hand around Cassie's shoulder. He shoved her gently toward the corridor leading to the bathroom. "Now do as Dani says and get cleaned up for supper."

"Mr. Montana, I hardly think it's wise to reassure the child that no one is going to take her away when, in fact, that may very well become necessary." Claudia's smile was thin. "For her own good, of course. I think it would be to everyone's benefit if you were to at least discuss the possibility with her."

Cassie gave Jake a panic-stricken look. Dani walked across to her swiftly and knelt down, giving her a hug. "It's all right, Cass," she said quietly. "No one's taking you anywhere."

"Promise?" Cassie whispered, her eyes wide and frightened.

"Promise." Cassie must have heard something in Dani's voice that reassured her, because she smiled tentatively. Dani smiled back. "Hands and face. With soap."

She waited until Cassie was out of sight, then stood up and faced Claudia furiously. "Just what the *hell* do you think you're doing, talking like that in front of a six-year-old? You've got her scared to death! And what gives you the right to walk in here uninvited and run roughshod over this family? I don't know how you got this job, lady, but I intend to report you all the way to the top. Your professional conduct stinks!"

"Dani . . ." Jake said warningly.

"I have all the authority I need," Claudia snapped. "My job is to ensure that child is—"

"That *child* has a name," Dani reminded her angrily. "And since when does your job entail bully tactics and intimidation?" She was half aware of Jake looming in the background, but knew she had gone so far beyond the point of no return that it was useless even to attempt retreating now. There would be no reconciliation, no smoothing of ruffled feathers. This was a fight to the death, and they both knew it.

Claudia smiled. "Rather than discuss my professional qualifications, perhaps you'd like to tell me who you are— and what your relationship is with Mr. Montana."

"That," Jake said angrily, "is none of your damn business!"

"Oh, it *is* my business," Claudia said haughtily, eyes triumphant as she went in for the kill. "The department doesn't care about a man's sex life, Mr. Montana. But they do expect him to be discreet. A man who brings his girlfriends home where they are an influence on his daughter's moral upbringing cannot be considered a fit father. I'm sure my—"

"I am *not* Jake's girlfriend," Dani snapped.

"No?" One elegant eyebrow lifted derisively, and Dani wondered just how long this woman had been standing behind them before she'd made her presence known. "Then perhaps you'd be so good as to tell me who you are."

"My name is—" She stopped dead, her mind racing with explanations, implications. She saw Claudia's little smirk, heard Jake draw in a breath to say something. "My name is Danielle Montana," she said without even thinking. "I'm Jake's . . . wife."

Seven

***

Dani distinctly heard Jake's sharp intake of breath and didn't dare look at him. Claudia simply stared at her, the shock on her face almost comical. Then she caught herself and started to turn toward Jake. But that slight hesitation was all Jake had needed. As smoothly as an ice skater catching his balance, he strolled across to Dani and draped his arm around her shoulders, giving Claudia the full benefit of his megawatt grin, the perfect image of the proud new husband.

"Well, this is certainly a surprise." Claudia's voice was rough with shock. "When did the happy event take place?"

"A week ago," Jake lied smoothly. "We had a quiet ceremony."

"Very," Dani managed to get out.

"Well, I . . . suppose there's no point in my staying." She looked as though she could have cheerfully killed both of them.

"It's been a pleasure," Jake drawled. "I'll show you out."

"No need. I know the way." She turned on her heel and strode across the room, back rigid.

The door closed behind her with a bang and Dani groaned. "I can't believe I said that," she whispered.

"That," Jake told her with a delighted laugh, "was some of the quickest thinking I've ever seen! Danielle Montana! I thought she was going to go through the floor!"

"And when she starts asking around town about Jake Montana's new wife?" Dani asked grimly. "What if she talks to Buster?" She closed her eyes. "My God, what a stupid thing to do!"

"She's got no reason to start asking around. And even if she does—so what? People get married quietly all the time. And don't forget I'm going to *be* married—legitimately married—before long anyway."

"And how are you going to explain the obvious differences between *this* Mrs. Montana and the one you're going to be squiring around in a few months?"

"I don't have to explain it to anyone," Jake said quietly.

"And that Schefer woman?"

"It'll be too late by then. Even if she wanted to make a case out of it, she couldn't." Jake chuckled. "You know, you reminded me of a lioness defending her family, keeping between me and that woman."

"I did not!" But Dani realized even as she said it that she'd done exactly that. She'd reacted instinctively, exactly like a lioness keeping herself between hunter and cub. She gave a tremulous laugh and looked up at Jake. "I guess I did get a little carried away. I'm sorry. I didn't mean to butt in, but she made me so *damn* mad! And then that crack about flaunting your girlfriend in front of Cassie..."

"I've never had anyone fight for me like that," he said softly. "It's always been Cass and me against the world. Except for Buster, there's never been anyone who cared before."

"I care," Dani heard herself whispering.

"Do you?" His eyes held hers, and she felt his fingers tighten on her shoulders. "Dani, I—"

"Is she gone, Daddy?"

The spell shattered. Jake stepped back, his hands falling from her shoulders, and Dani discovered that sometime during the past few seconds she'd stopped breathing. She drew in a deep breath, feeling a little shaky, trying to decide if she was glad or disappointed that Jake hadn't been able to finish what he'd started to say. There had been a moment, staring up into those vibrant blue eyes, when she'd been absolutely certain he was going to say he loved her. And if he had . . . oh, lord, if he *had*, she'd have blurted out heaven knows what kind of rubbish in return.

This whole situation had gotten completely out of hand. He had her so mixed up about what she felt, or thought she felt, she didn't know if she was coming or going. He didn't love her, regardless of what he might find himself believing. And she didn't love him. Her mind knew this particular Ideal Man was for someone else, but her heart hadn't figured that out yet. It was still dizzy with discovery, and unless she could keep it under control, it was going to drive her crazy.

" . . . help you set the table?"

Dani blinked, came to and realized that Cassie was looking up at her expectantly. "You sure can, Cass. But I thought you said you were going to wash your face."

"I did!"

Dani had to laugh, noticing that she had indeed washed a small area around her mouth. The rest of her face, however, was still smeared with red paint. "The idea is to wash the *whole* face, honey."

"But I don't wanna ruin my war paint! Cochise did it. He said every squiggle means a bad word in Blackfoot."

"Every squiggle is going to mean a bad word in English if you don't quit arguing," Jake told her calmly. "Go!"

She went, muttering under her breath every step of the way. Jake smiled at Dani. "Just what I need—a daughter who can swear fluently in English *and* Blackfoot."

Dani laughed and started to follow Cassie. "Look on the bright side—no one will understand a word she's saying!"

"I'm really glad you're stayin' with us while Gran'pa's in the hospital." Cassie was leaning across the big kitchen table, feet swinging. "Aren't you glad she's stayin', Daddy?"

"Wouldn't have it any other way."

Dani gave Jake a shrewd look, but he was seemingly engrossed in the farm magazine he was reading. He'd had his nose in it all evening, and she was beginning to wonder if it was really that interesting or if he was simply using it as an excuse to be here in the kitchen with her and Cassie instead of outside helping Jesse and Cochise.

She had Cassie's angel costume spread across the table. Eyeing the outfit thoughtfully, she picked up another sequin. "Jesse says they'll have the duck pond finished tomorrow."

"Not a moment too soon," Jake muttered. "Damn things are underfoot every time I turn around."

Dani knotted the thread and bit it off, hiding her smile. Buster's pet ducks were a source of constant irritation to Jake, as were his grandfather's dozen or so laying hens and the four big geese that paraded around like royalty. But she'd noticed that it was Jake who fed them faithfully every day, and Jake who, more often than not, could be found inspecting the henhouse for predator-size holes.

"This is a cattle ranch," Cassie piped up in a fair imitation of Jake's voice, "not a damn poultry farm!"

Jake shot his daughter a sharp glance that she blithely ignored, and Dani gave a sputter of laughter that earned her one as sharp. "What did you promise me about swearing, Cass?" she asked quietly.

Cassie gave an embarrassed wriggle. "Sorry."

Dani caught Jake's amused smile across Cassie's golden head and smiled back comfortably.

Perhaps a little *too* comfortably, she found herself musing as Jake turned back to his reading and she picked up another sequin. It was disconcerting how easily she'd fitted into life here on Silvercreek. It had been four days since Jake had asked her to stay, and already her other life, the one she'd left behind in Toronto, seemed as remote as a dream.

She'd caught herself more than once standing at the sink watching the play of shadow and sunlight on the snow-tipped peaks of the Cariboo Range, trying to remember exactly what the city looked like. Her glass-walled condo overlooking the inner harbor, the trendy little Church Street restaurants, the high-fashion stores on Bloor Street West . . . all had faded from memory.

She glanced at Jake, who was still reading his magazine. He looked very relaxed, sipping his evening coffee after a full day's work and a good supper.

It was disconcerting how easily she'd fitted into *his* life, too. They'd fallen into an easy, relaxed routine almost from the beginning. Jake would be up first, and by the time she got to the kitchen, there would be a steaming mug of coffee awaiting her, rich with fresh cream the way she liked it. Sometimes she'd make breakfast while he got Cassie up and dressed, and sometimes they'd prepare it together, chatting about this and that as they moved in comfortable harmony in the big kitchen. Cochise and Jesse would hit the kitchen door precisely at seven, half starved, and she and Cassie would spend their breakfast talking while Jake and his men planned their day.

Evenings were more relaxed. She'd have supper on the table by six sharp, and by seven, after Jesse and Cochise had wandered off to their bunkhouse, she, Jake and Cassie would wash the dishes and clean up. Jake would often put the stereo on and settle in by the fire with a book, and she and Cassie would work on the angel costume or Cassie's lines for her play. Then Cassie would go to bed, and the evening would be theirs.

They talked, mostly. The hours would slip by unnoticed as they rambled from topic to topic, completely relaxed in each other's company. The fire would die down to a whisper, wafting the sweet scent of pine and alder through the air until finally she or Jake would notice how late it was and gather up the empty coffee mugs and carry them into the kitchen. They'd check the house together, get the assorted animals settled and turn off the lights. Then they'd stroll down the corridor and say good-night at the foot of the stairs.

It had gotten to be almost a game that Dani would start upstairs and Jake would reach over the railing and tug her gently into his arms. He'd kiss her lightly, never pressing what both of them knew to be a volatile situation.

They'd simply stand there, Dani tucked in Jake's undemanding embrace, the house silent and still around them. Then he'd kiss her again, letting his mouth linger on hers as long as he dared before letting his arms fall away. She'd slip upstairs wordlessly, pausing at the top landing to share one last smile before he, too, turned and walked down to his bedroom. It was always a special time, a brief, wistful sharing of the unexpected tenderness that had grown between them. Neither of them ever spoke of it, yet Dani never doubted that Jake looked forward to those few quiet minutes every evening as much as she did.

"More coffee?"

Dani blinked. Jake was standing beside her with the coffee pot poised over her mug, and she nodded, realizing she'd been sitting there, needle in one hand and a sequin in the other, her mind a thousand miles away. "Sorry. I was thinking about...how to fasten these wings on so they don't droop."

"Uh-huh." He filled her mug, his eyes meeting hers for an amused second as though knowing she'd no more been thinking about angel wings than he had. "Binder twine and baling wire should do it."

"It would certainly add authenticity," Dani told him dryly. "After all, the play *is* called *Heaven Loves Cowgirls*."

"I was s'posed to be the cowgirl," Cassie spoke up, "but Ms. Wilson said I'd make a better heavenly angel." Her expression made her own opinion quite clear. "But at least I don't gotta be a troll like that dumb Robby Jacobsen."

Jake nearly choked on a mouthful of hot coffee.

"Don't *have* to be, not 'don't gotta,'" Dani said with a chuckle. "Is this Robby Jacobsen really as awful as you let on, or are you indulging in a bit of hormonal hyperbole?"

"Hormonal *what*?" Cassie wrinkled her nose.

"Mild exaggeration," Dani explained with a smile. "It's something we women often do when faced with a situation—or a man—we don't quite know what to do with."

"I know what I'd like to do with Robby Jacobsen," Cassie told her darkly. "Do you know what he did yesterday at play school? He sneaked up and stole the picture I was drawing. And he said he wouldn't give it back unless I kissed him!"

Jake looked up. "How old is this kid?"

"Jake," Dani said soothingly. Starting to stitch on another sequin, she looked at Cassie. "And did you?"

"No way! I punched his lights out!"

Jake rolled his eyes heavenward, then went back to his reading. Dani smiled. "Well, true love doesn't always run smoothly. Next time Robby pulls a stunt like that, just smile sweetly and tell him you'd rather kiss a frog or a toad than a troll. Then go on as though nothing happened. I can guarantee you'll have him begging for mercy in a week."

"I'd rather just sock him," Cassie muttered. She looked at Dani. "Do you like kissin'?"

Dani sucked her breath in as she rammed the needle into the end of her finger. "I . . . well, yes. Usually." She sucked her punctured finger, ignoring Jake's interested gaze. "It can be nice. I think it helps to be a bit older than six, though, Cassie. It's something you sort of grow into."

"Like a brassiere?"

"Like a *what*?" Jake asked in astonishment.

"A brassiere." Cassie turned to look at him. "You know, Daddy! It's one of them things that—"

"I *know* what a brassiere is," Jake assured her hastily. "I haven't heard that word in about a hundred years, that's all. I thought they were just called bras now."

Cassie shrugged. "I dunno. That dumb Robby Jacobsen says—"

"I'm going to kill that kid," Jake growled. "Now I know why fathers talk about locking their daughters into nunneries until they turn twenty-one!"

"It only gets worse," Dani told him sweetly.

Jake looked singularly unhappy.

"Do you like it when Daddy kisses you?" Cassie asked.

Dani, very glad she'd put the needle down, didn't dare look in Jake's direction. "I, umm..."

"I seen you last night. You *seemed* to like it."

Dani took a deep breath. "I...well..."

"Well, Ms. Ross?" Jake drawled.

"Isn't it your bedtime, Cassie?" Dani asked.

"Not until you answer the question!" Cassie grinned up at her. "Isn't that right, Daddy? She has to tell!"

"That's right, Ms. Ross. We're both mighty interested."

Dani gave him a ferocious look that only made him grin. "It's better than kissing trolls," she admitted finally. "Or even frogs, for that matter. And it's *saw*, not 'seen'. Now off to bed!"

"Promises, promises," Jake murmured.

Dani gave him another glare as she got to her feet and started gathering up Cassie's costume. "It's your turn to read tonight, cowboy. *Black Beauty*, chapter six."

It was nearly half an hour later when Dani heard Jake padding down the stairs from Cassie's room, then down the long back corridor toward his own main-floor bedroom.

The shower came on a few minutes later, and Dani finished cleaning up the kitchen, then put on a fresh pot of coffee. The sound of voices wafted through the kitchen window. She glanced out and raised her hand in greeting as Jesse and Cochise walked across the yard. They both got into Jesse's old yellow pickup and a moment later tore up the lane toward the main road, radio blaring.

"Lock up your daughters," she murmured with a laugh. "Trouble's on its way tonight!"

She had just finished adding a couple of pine logs to the fire Jake had lit earlier when she heard him go into the kitchen, whistling softly. Kicking her shoes off, she sat down on the big deep-cushioned sofa, propped her feet on the coffee table, ankles crossed, and waited for Jake to bring in the coffee.

It was almost like being married, she found herself thinking suddenly. They'd fallen into this comfortable evening routine like two people who had been together for years instead of a few days. Like two people who had an entire lifetime ahead of them, years of fireside chats and shared dreams and laughter. . . .

Dani caught her wayward thoughts firmly, unnerved at how easily they got away from her these days. She'd caught herself daydreaming like this before, thoughts rambling in all sorts of crazy directions, and it was starting to worry her. It was almost as though some part of her had started to believe the lie she'd told Claudia Schefer, that some tiny, wistful part of her really wanted to *be* Mrs. Jake Montana.

Which was ridiculous. It was just a game, after all. A temporary, stopgap measure that didn't mean a thing to either of them. After all, if she'd thought for even a minute there was any danger of either Jake or her confusing make-believe with reality, she'd have left days ago.

"You got a toothache, or just thinking hard?"

Dani realized she'd been staring into the fireplace and frowning deeply. "Thinking, believe it or not." She looked up, her heart giving that odd little leap it always did when those deep blue eyes met hers.

Even expecting to see him there, she still had to catch her breath at the picture he made. Naked to the waist, sun-bronzed torso glistening with stray beads of water, he was padding silently toward her through the shadows of the fire-lit room like a large golden-limbed cat. He hadn't bothered buttoning the waistband of his jeans, and it gaped slightly, offering a suggestive glimpse of suntanned skin above the glint of the zipper that Dani found distinctly unsettling.

"Was that Jesse's truck I heard?"

"Yes." She suddenly realized he was carrying a wine bottle and two glasses instead of the coffee. "I don't know how they can work as hard as they do all day, then go into town nearly every night to do things I don't even want to think about, drag themselves in at two in the morning, then get up at six and do it all over again."

"It's what being young, single and male is all about." Jake set the glasses down. "Especially the *young* part. Unlike us old guys who prefer to stay home in front of the fire with a beautiful, sexy woman and a bottle of good wine."

Dani smiled. "What's the occasion?"

The cork came out of the bottle with a soft pop and Jake glanced up at her and grinned lazily. "The kid's in bed, the boys are in town—we have the place to ourselves. Since when does a man need an excuse to share a quiet evening and a glass of wine with his lady?"

There was something about the easy way he talked that made Dani catch her breath, and for one mad instant she found herself wishing it were true, that she was "his lady."

"Mrs. Montana."

A wineglass appeared in front of her, and Dani stared at it for a moment before realizing it was for her. She took it, then smiled. "I'd hoped you'd forgotten about that. You haven't mentioned it once since that wretched woman left."

Jake filled her glass with white wine. "Just because I haven't mentioned it doesn't mean I'd forgotten." He looked at her intently. "As a matter of fact, I think about it a lot."

Dani's heart did a quick double cartwheel. "Oh."

His mouth curved around a coaxing smile. "That's the best you can do? Just *oh*?"

Dani looked up at him, knowing that something was happening here that shouldn't *be* happening. That they had agreed would *not* happen. She had her mouth half-open to tell him that when she found herself wondering instead if he had any idea of the image he made standing there half-naked in the firelight, hair tousled and damp.

"To us."

His soft baritone wrenched her back into the present. Dani swallowed, her throat suddenly dry as she tried to get her treacherous thoughts under control. "Us?" she echoed idiotically.

Jake's laugh wrapped around her like melted chocolate. "Us. You and me. The marriage that never was."

"Oh." Again, as answers went, her response was scarcely adequate, but it was the best she could manage. She realized he was standing there expectantly, glass held out, and she hastily tipped hers against his. "To us. *You*, I mean! To you."

He dropped onto the sofa beside her, draping one arm negligently across the back as he turned to face her. "Well, buttercup, which is it?"

"To you," Dani said firmly. "To you and . . . and Caroline."

Something flickered across Jake's strong features. He frowned and reached out to catch her hand as she lifted the glass to her mouth. "I don't want to drink to that."

"But—"

"I want this one for us," he said quietly. "These past few days have been magic. I don't want to write them off this easily."

"Jake . . ."

"Humor me."

Dani swallowed a sigh. "All right. A toast to you and me."

She lifted her glass, and Jake gently clinked his against it. His eyes were shadowed and deep, and she felt her heart tighten while she wondered if it were possible to get drunk merely on the promise of wine. "Oh, Jake, what are we doing?"

"Just having a drink together."

But his voice said everything the words didn't, and Dani wasn't surprised when he took the glass from her. She tried to shake her head in denial, but he cupped her cheek in his hand and lifted her face, and in the next instant his mouth was gliding slowly along hers.

"Jake—Jake, we can't do this..."

"One kiss," he murmured, his tongue outlining the curve of her lips. "Just one kiss. For the toast..."

"But...but we didn't even drink the toast!" she said desperately, knowing she should be stopping him before things got out of hand.

"I did," Jake murmured huskily. "Drink it from me, Dani...."

And then his mouth was over hers, soft and deliciously warm, and she parted her lips and tasted the sweetness of the wine. His tongue captured hers and moved slowly against it, each wet, slippery caress sending her senses spinning ever nearer that bright, dangerous edge.

She put her hands on his shoulders, intending to push him away, but drew him nearer instead. She ran her hands along the slope of his shoulders to his neck and cradled it, then somehow found the strength to turn her mouth from under his. But instead of pulling away she moved her cheek against his smoothly shaven one and was enveloped in the heady scent of shampoo and soap and warm male skin.

"Oh, my God, Jake, this is insane!"

"Absolutely," he murmured, nuzzling her throat, her neck.

"Jake, I'm serious...we shouldn't be doing this!"

"I know."

"Jake...!"

"Wouldn't it be the damnedest thing if *we* fell in love," he whispered, his tongue drawing wet spirals up one side of her throat to her ear. "If you and I beat the odds and made it come true?"

"Don't be crazy!" Dani turned her face and found his mouth with delicious ease. "We know better." His mouth opened and she kissed him urgently. "Whatever this is, it can't be love." One of his hands was on her breast, and she moaned in pleasure at the sensations his work-roughened palm drew from her even through her cotton shirt.

"Whatever it is, I like it," he murmured. "I like it a lot."

"Jake," she gasped, "this isn't supposed to be happening."

"It's exactly what's supposed to be happening, Dani. Nothing that feels this right can be wrong."

"I have a responsibility to my client," she whispered. His mouth probed hers, and she nibbled his lower lip and ran her hands across his broad shoulders. His skin was smooth and hot. Even knowing she was breaking every rule in every book ever written, she couldn't stop herself from touching him. She ran her hands down his chest, heard his quick intake of breath as she brushed his taut nipples with her fingertips, then drew her fingernails lightly across his stomach and along the waistband of his jeans.

"I'm your client," he reminded her in a husky growl that made Dani's toes curl. His eyes were narrowed and smoky, and she could feel the powerful thump of his heart against her fingertips. "And you're not doing anything your client doesn't want...."

"Oh, Jake..." It was no more than a breath as his mouth dropped over hers and he kissed her with a deep, drugging intensity, sending whatever protest she'd been about to make spinning away.

She felt him tug her blouse out of her jeans, then sighed as his fingers curved around her bare back and ran slowly up

to her shoulders then down again. The narrow band of her
bra parted, and her breasts filled his hands. He groaned
against her mouth, touching her gently yet knowledgeably,
drawing the most incredible sensations from her.

She held her breath as he moved past the waistband of her
jeans and ran the knuckle of his thumb slowly down the
stitching of the zipper. Dani whispered his name, her voice
catching on a soft moan as he pressed gently against her,
tracing the curve of the seam as it ran between her thighs.

"Jake...!" It was half protest, half question, and he
murmured something against her ear as he lay back against
the mound of pillows, holding her so that she was lying full-
length along his lean body, legs tangled with his.

He cupped her face in his hands and lifted it, drawing his
tongue from the soft indentation at the base of her throat up
to her chin. Then his mouth was under hers. He kissed her
hungrily, and she felt all the last tendrils of hesitation vanish in the magic of his mouth and hands.

The ache of desire that had been tolerable until then
blossomed into something that could no longer be denied,
as strong and explicit as the lean male body moving coax-
ingly under hers. She caressed him, silken skin teasing taut
male flesh until both of them were half-wild with the promise. Jake ran his hands down her back and cupped the swell
of her bottom, pressing her against him. His mouth plun-
dered hers, and she could taste his desire in her throat.

"Daddy?"

The small, sleepy voice coming from somewhere in the
shadows behind them took Jake so much by surprise that he
froze. Slowly, not daring to move, he took a deep, steady-
ing breath. "What is it, Cass?" he asked very calmly, swallowing.

Calmly Dani lifted her head from the hollow of his throat
and sat up as Cassie padded around the end of the sofa.
"Hi. Can't sleep?" she asked the little girl.

Cassie didn't seem the least bit surprised to find them together. She shook her head sleepily, her floppy-eared stuffed rabbit tucked under one arm. "I had a bad dream."

"Is it okay now?" Dani reached out and brushed Cassie's hair from her cheek.

Cassie nodded, and Jake managed to unclench his teeth enough to smile. "Why don't you go back up to bed, half-pint, and I'll come up in a couple of minutes and tuck you in again?"

"I think there's something bad in the closet."

"Would you like to sleep in your daddy's bed for a while?" Dani asked softly.

"Can I, Daddy?" Cassie asked, smiling drowsily.

"Go on in, sweetie. I'll run upstairs and check the closet in a few minutes, okay?"

"Okay." She nodded, more asleep than awake, and turned to pad off across the room again.

"My God." Jake released a tight breath between his teeth and lay there for a few minutes, not daring to move.

"Are you all right?" Dani whispered.

"No." He drew one leg up, wincing. "I may never be all right again."

Dani laughed quietly, but even that slight motion made Jake groan. "Serves you right for breaking the first rule of parenthood. Thou shalt never make love in rooms without locked doors."

"Believe me, it's going to be a long time before I forget."

"Can I get up?"

Jake gritted his teeth and nodded. "If you do it very carefully."

She extricated herself from the sofa, looking very tousled and flushed. Averting her eyes from him, she refastened her bra under her blouse.

Jake touched her shoulder. "How about you?"

"I'm fine."

He slowly sat up and swung his feet to the floor. Sitting there quietly, elbows on knees, he turned his head to look at

Dani. "I'm sorry. You're right—that *was* a damn stupid thing to do." He got to his feet and fastened the top of his jeans, swearing gently under his breath. Dani was sitting on the big hassock by the fire, staring into the flames, arms wrapped around herself.

He kissed the top of her head. "I'll be back in a few minutes."

Cassie was already asleep by the time he got to his bedroom, curled up in the middle of the big bed like an elf. He gazed down at her for a moment or two, then tucked the sheet and blankets around her shoulders and left her there, pausing to smooth her hair back from her warm cheek. She stirred slightly, smiling in her sleep, and Jake laughed quietly.

"Your timing's lousy, half-pint," he whispered, "but I love you anyway."

Dani was still sitting when he walked back into the living room. He sat behind her, straddling the hassock, and wrapped his arms around her. "She's asleep, but I decided the best thing was to leave her there. So why don't we take the glasses and wine and retire to your room and pick this discussion up where we left off?"

"No, Jake." Dani slipped free of his embrace and stood up, rubbing her arms as though she were cold. "Damn it, I—" She shook her head and looked around at him. "I don't know what happened tonight, Jake. I'd like to blame it on the wine, but I didn't have any." She gave a sob of laughter. "So maybe it was the firelight, or the... oh, hell, I don't know."

She wheeled away and Jake sighed, feeling an odd emptiness wash through him. "It's been four days, Jake."

"I can count." He'd meant it teasingly, but the words had come out harsh and stiff and he sensed more than saw Dani look around at him. "I've had no luck finding anyone to come in. You know that."

"Have you been trying?" Her voice sounded muffled, almost angry.

"Yes, damn it, I have been trying!" He leaped to his feet and picked up his glass of wine, finishing it in one swallow. He felt restless and angry for no reason at all, his emotions frayed like cheap cotton.

"What about that Williams Lake woman who called yesterday?"

"She can't stay more than two weeks. Her daughter's having a baby or something and she'll be in Winnipeg all summer."

"Two weeks will give you time to find someone else."

Jake stared at the window, seeing nothing but reflections of the room behind him. It looked warm and inviting, but it was an illusion, as was the woman standing by the fire—all illusions. "Are you really in that much of a hurry to leave?" He didn't expect an answer and wasn't surprised when she said nothing. Sighing, he stared into his empty glass.

"No." It was just a whisper, then there was a feathery touch of fingertips along his shoulders. He heard her sigh as she slipped her arms around his waist and rested her cheek on his back. "Jake, if Cassie hadn't come down, we'd be on the sofa making love right now. And I just don't know if I . . . can handle that."

"I've got news for you, buttercup," he told her harshly. "I didn't drag you over there kicking and screaming."

"Jake, stop it!" She wrenched her arms away from him and strode around to face him angrily. "I'm not blaming you—we both wanted it to happen. But it shouldn't have happened. Don't you see? Marion Wainwright-Syms is paying me to find you, not fall in love with you myself!"

Jake went very still. "Fall in love with?"

She stared at him, then suddenly flushed. "That's not what I meant. I meant she's not paying me to *make* love with you."

"You said *fall* in love with," he reminded her, suddenly curious as to what she *had* meant.

Dani seemed flustered, her cheeks pink. "I know what I said," she snapped. "It was just a slip, that's all. For heaven's sake, you don't have to look at me like that. I'm not going to do something stupid like fall in love with you and . . . and make this all messy. I told you I don't even *believe* in love."

"Yeah, so you did." For some reason he didn't find her assurance as satisfying as he should have. Frowning, he put the glass down, then walked over to where she was standing and put his hands on her shoulders, turning her to face him. "Marion Wainwright-Syms has nothing to do with this, buttercup. Not her or her sister or that ad Buster answered or any of it. This is something between you and me."

"Jake . . ." she said warningly.

"I know, I know." He held his hands up wearily, letting her step away. "I'm not supposed to be thinking this way. But damn it, Dani, I can't help the way I feel. My *mind* knows you're off-limits, but the rest of me says different." *My heart says differently,* he nearly found himself saying, realizing with a shock that it was true. It had been so long since that particular part of him had said anything that it disconcerted him to discover it was still capable.

"I know." She frowned, looking a little impatient, a little confused. "I was supposed to come up here, interview you, sign some papers if everything worked out and zip back to Toronto. None of this—" her gesture took in the entire house "—was supposed to happen! I wasn't supposed to wind up caring!"

Jake's heart gave a startling leap. He wanted to hear her say more—to tell him how *much* she cared, how important Silvercreek Ranch and Jake Montana had become to her.

Then, abruptly, he caught himself. This wasn't real. She'd said it herself. It was nothing more than a bit of springtime mountain magic that wouldn't last the summer, and pretending it would ever be anything else was sheer madness.

"I'll call the woman from Williams Lake back tomorrow," he said quietly. "But I'd appreciate it if you'd stay until she can get up here—another day, maybe. Besides," he added with a faint smile, "you can't leave before Cassie's play tomorrow night."

She looked up, her eyes catching his for a heartbeat. "Not after all the work I put into that costume."

"Yeah..." There seemed to be something unsaid hanging between them, and their eyes held for a long time.

Then she let her gaze slide away and she turned and walked slowly toward the door. "Good night, Jake."

Wouldn't it be funny if we fell in love. His own voice came back to him, mocking him gently from the silences of his mind. *Wouldn't it be funny....*

Eight

There was no point in lying anymore. Lies wouldn't make reality go away, so she might as well simply admit it and get it over with.

She was in love with Jake Montana.

Dani rested her forehead on the cool glass of her bedroom window, staring out across the hills to the moon-silvered mountains beyond. How it had happened, she had no idea. She just knew that she'd been fighting the realization for what seemed like days, and that tonight it had hit her with such crystalline clarity that it was pointless even trying to deny it.

"Terrific." She took a deep breath and turned away from the window. "Just terrific."

Her small bedroom, decorated in red and white country prints, rag rugs and pine furniture, was cozy and warm, bathed in the buttery glow from the bedside lamp. She walked over to the bed and sat on the edge, curling her bare toes into the thick rug. Miss Margaret, the gray-and-white cat that had taken to sleeping on her feet every night, sat on the end of the bed, feet and tail tucked tidily under, purring very softly.

"This wasn't supposed to happen," Dani whispered. She ran her fingers through the cat's velvet fur. "Can you imagine trying to explain it to Caroline? 'Well, yes, as a matter of fact I *did* find your Ideal Man, Miss Wainwright. But I've fallen head over heels in love with him and have decided to keep him myself, sorry.'" She gave a snort of laughter that made Miss Margaret's ears tilt back disapprovingly.

Lying back across the bed, she stared at the ceiling, torn between bursting into tears or laughing with the sheer joy of what she was feeling. Just to be *feeling* again, that was the magical part. Feeling things she thought had been lost to her forever. It was exciting and wonderful and terrifying all at once, and she had no idea what it meant.

Except that she was going to have to put the finishing touches on a marriage between the man *she* loved and another woman and she was going to have to smile while doing it. It was the price she was going to pay for falling in love with a man who, by his own admission, couldn't love her back.

Miss Margaret looked at the door expectantly and Dani stiffened, hearing soft footsteps on the stairs. Then she realized it was just Jake carrying Cassie to her own bedroom. Miss Margaret yawned and stretched out on her side, one paw curled around her nose, and Dani got up to open the window so that the cat could come and go during the night without waking her.

She heard the door to Cassie's bedroom close gently, then footsteps along the corridor. They paused just outside her door, and Dani froze, her heart racing. He was out there, standing silently and still in the darkness, just the thickness of the door between them. She closed her eyes, then opened them again to stare down at the brass knob glowing like gold just inches from her hand.

All she had to do was turn it. There would be no need for words. One look was all it would take. He'd step through the door and they'd tumble across the bed, hands and bodies seeking what they already knew by heart. In moments he'd slip between her thighs, both of them so ready for each other that to prolong it would simply be torture. Her body would cry out and his would answer and soon there would be nothing but the sound of their hearts racing, the whisper of flesh on flesh.

She squeezed her eyes closed, her body aching for his touch, and she could taste the salt of her own tears. "Jake..."

"Dani?" It was so softly spoken that she thought for a moment that she'd merely imagined it.

She held her breath, picturing him out there, so close she could almost hear his gentle breathing. She had her mouth open to answer before she caught herself and swallowed the words that would bring him to her. It was pointless to even pretend it could be anything more than what it *would* be—one night of incredible but loveless passion. Worse, she'd be breaking her word. He *trusted* her. She'd told him in no uncertain terms that she didn't believe in love and he'd believed her—he would come to her bed thinking she understood that, trusting her not to complicate it.

She thought she heard a sigh. A loose board creaked gently as he shifted his weight. Then she heard him move away and pad quietly down the stairs. She didn't realize she was still holding her breath until she slowly released it. For one rash moment she was tempted to fling the door open and call out to him, but what was the point? Leaving was going to be hard enough as it was. Why torture herself further by allowing herself a taste of the magic she could never have? Sharing another day with him, being with him tomorrow night at Cassie's concert—that was the best she could hope for. Then she was going to leave. And, in about a hundred years or so when she'd finally gotten him out of her system, she'd look back at this whole fiasco and laugh.

* * *

"Dani," Jake bawled outside the bedroom for the third time in as many minutes, "are you two coming or not? We're going to be late if you don't—"

"In a minute!" Dani tightened the bow in Cassie's hair, then stood back to admire her handiwork. "Your father's going to drive me crazy before this night's over."

"He's been actin' weird all day. Cochise said he was sitting out by the corral for *hours*, not doing nothing—anything, I mean. Just sitting and looking at the mountains, like he was thinking about something important." Cassie slipped her a sly glance. "Jesse says he was prob'ly thinking about you."

"I doubt that," Dani said calmly. "I imagine he was thinking about Buster. There—take a look."

Cassie took a couple of skips toward the full-length mirror and stood there for a moment, frowning as though not recognizing the little girl gazing back. Which wasn't surprising, Dani thought with a smile. Cassie looked like the angel she would be portraying later that evening, dressed in a pale blue dress with a darker blue velvet bodice and matching bolero jacket that Dani had unearthed in the back of the closet. Cassie had voluntarily dug out a pair of matching blue shoes, which, to Dani's relief, still fit, and another search had turned up the matching velvet ribbon that now adorned Cassie's hair. Dani had drawn a thick strand back from each temple and secured it with a bow, and the rest cascaded around Cassie's shoulders in a mass of golden curls.

"You're beautiful," Dani told her softly.

Cassie's cheeks glowed, and she broke into a wide smile, her eyes meeting Dani's in the glass. "You look beautiful, too."

Dani laughed. "Well, thank you. Are you ready to let your father see? He's pacing out there like a lion."

"Yeah!" Cassie's eyes sparkled. "Bet he's surprised!"

"I have a feeling he just might be." Dani went to the door and stepped out.

Jake was leaning against the doorframe, eyeing his watch impatiently. "It's about time you—" He stopped and looked at her wordlessly, his gaze traveling from head to foot and gave a long, low whistle. "You look like a million bucks!"

To her surprise, Dani felt herself blush. She'd taken extra care with her hair and makeup tonight, and had fretted over what to wear for hours. She'd finally settled on cream-colored wool slacks and a pale pink angora sweater stitched with pearls and satin appliqués that set off her dark eyes and hair.

"It's not too much for a school play, is it?" she asked doubtfully. "I don't want to stand out like a city slicker."

"Lady," Jake murmured, "you'd stand out no matter where you were!"

"You ain't seen nothin' yet, cowboy," she told him with a laugh. "Cassie...?"

As his daughter stepped from around the door, Jake's face registered astonishment. Cassie pirouetted, gazing shyly up at her father. "Dani thinks I'm beautiful. Do you think I'm beautiful, Daddy?"

Jake dropped down on one knee, shaking his head as he gazed at her in wonder. "You're always beautiful, Cass," he said quietly. "But tonight—well, sweetheart, tonight you're something else again! I'm going to be the envy of the Cariboo when I walk into that school auditorium with you two beside me."

"Oh, Daddy!" Cassie giggled. Then she took another look at herself in the mirror. "It looks okay, I guess. But if that dumb Robby Jacobsen says anything, I'll fix him good!"

"Dani, I'm so glad you came tonight!" Beth Wilson gave Dani a quick embrace, her face glowing. "I don't think I've seen Cassie look prettier—or happier. She's walking on air.

And, for that matter, so is Jake. And you sure you two aren't...?"

"I'm sure," Dani said swiftly, praying she wasn't going to ruin her denial by blushing. "And thanks for picking Buster up at the hospital and bringing him down. I don't know how you managed it alone, between the cast and the wheelchair. Jake was going up to help, but you were already here."

"It was Buster's idea," Beth admitted with a laugh. "He wanted to see Cassie's face when she walked in and saw him. She's been fretting about his missing the play ever since he was hurt."

"Well, you're right, she *is* walking on air. For the moment, anyway. I don't think it's hit her yet that this is the big night, that in twenty minutes she's going to be performing in front of a live audience."

"It hasn't hit any of them yet," Beth assured her. She gazed around the crowded room where a dozen or so excited children and their mothers were putting the finishing touches on costumes and makeup. The hubbub had been rising steadily in volume until the air practically vibrated with it. "In about ten minutes half my theatrical company will be throwing up and the other half will be in tears, and it's going to be a madhouse of crying children and hysterical mothers back here. I'd invite you to stay, but I don't think Jake is finished showing you off yet." She smiled at someone over Dani's shoulder, and Dani wasn't surprised when a moment later Jake's hand settled casually on her waist. "You can have her back now, Jake. We got Cassie into her costume without incident."

"No fistfights yet?" Jake looking around interestedly. A couple of the women saw him and waved, eyeing Dani curiously, and he returned their greetings. Cassie, who stood on the other side of the room, was being fussed over by a couple of motherly looking women. She beamed at him, looking every inch the angel she was, and Jake gave her a thumbs-up that made her glow.

"Nary a one," Dani told him with a grin. "Cass even helped Robby Jacobsen with his troll costume. The poor kid's got so many stars in his eyes he'll be walking into the sets all night."

"Is Buster all right?" Beth asked. "Not getting too tired, is he? His doctors said two hours were about the most he should be up and about."

Jake smiled. "He's fine, Beth. Tom Donaldson's widow was fussing over him when I left."

"Oh, she was, was she?" Beth's voice was crisp. "Well, we'll see about that. Excuse me, I'll be right back." She strode toward the door leading out into the crowded auditorium.

"I think poor Tom Donaldson's widow has met her match," Dani said with a laugh, glancing up at Jake. "You did that on purpose!"

He grinned. "I figure a woman has a right to know when someone's moving in on her man."

"I see."

"I saw Mason Ives talking to you a few minutes ago. He seemed pretty friendly."

Dani shrugged as she strolled toward the door. "He was just telling me about his law practice, and he happened to mention he gets out to Toronto quite often."

"Oh, he does, does he?" Jake said in a tone very similar to Beth Wilson's. He strode along silently at Dani's side, jaw set.

She slipped him a curious sidelong glance. *Now* what was going on? One moment he'd been the laughing, teasing Jake Montana she'd fallen in love with, and an eye blink later he was like a bear with a sore paw. Or a bear whose territorial prerogative had just been threatened. For a man who kept his heart locked behind closed doors, he was behaving very strangely.

"And Cliff Zeretski? I suppose he was telling you all about his herd of prize *Blonde d'Aquitaine* cattle, was he?"

"He said he had a small herd imported from France. I found it quite fascinating."

"He certainly seemed to find *you* fascinating," Jake muttered. "He was practically drooling."

Dani gave him a sharp look. They seemed to be involved in some complicated game of strategems and wits—only she didn't even know what the damn rules were! "If I didn't know better, I'd say you were exhibiting all the classic signs of jealousy. But that would be silly, wouldn't it? Considering there's nothing to be jealous *of*, I mean."

The words were quiet, but they had an edge to them that made Jake narrow his eyes. Why did she have to keep reminding him there was nothing between them? He was all too aware of the fact! Hell, he'd spent most of the day trying to get it through his thick skull, trying to forget the taste and feel of her, the scent of her hair, her skin. And then when she'd stepped out of that room tonight looking like everything a man's dreams were made of...

Not looking at her, he shrugged his shoulders to loosen the tight muscles across them. "Yeah," he said in a rough voice. "So you keep telling me."

Damn it, what was the matter with him? Ten minutes ago, looking across the crowded room and seeing Ives talking with her, he'd been on the verge of going over and planting his fist squarely in the young lawyer's handsome face. Which didn't make a lot of sense.

Dani was right. There was no reason for him to be jealous. She wasn't his woman. She was just out here doing her job, and the fact that *he* was having difficulty keeping things in perspective didn't mean he could go around punching out every man who gave her a second look.

He wrenched open the door to the auditorium. A wave of noise hit them, so loud that it was almost solid, and he stood there for a moment, staring out at the crowd. Most of them were friends. People he'd known all his life, people he'd gone to school with, grown up with. He'd dated half the women, had drunk beer and fished and fought with the men

who were now their husbands. The older ones had watched
him grow up, and the younger ones knew him as Mr. Montana and treated him with a respect that always amused him.
Mothers with unmarried daughters considered him fair
game, and there were two or three married women out there
who had made subtle, though unmistakable, passes at him.

And yet, at times, he was completely alone. Even with
Buster and Cassie around, he sometimes felt the chill of
loneliness, a chill that Dani's presence in his house and his
life had banished utterly. She'd filled the rooms of his home
and the spaces of his heart with a warmth and companion-
ship he'd never dreamed could be his, and he hated thinking what it was going to be like when she left and took the
sun with her.

He suddenly realized that she was looking at him oddly.
He stepped back to let her through the door, then fell into
step beside her silently.

The small auditorium was packed with laughing, chat-
tering people, all of them taking advantage of the evening
to catch up on their visiting. The whole community had
obviously turned out for Beth Wilson's play, and he found
himself fielding greetings left and right. But he edged Dani
through the crowd without stopping, not caring that his
reticence was going to fuel as much speculation as the
beautiful out-of-town woman at his side.

Dani, to his relief, didn't seem particularly perturbed by
the unapologetic scrutiny she'd received all evening. Coming from a small farming community herself, she probably
understood the stir it had caused to have one of the few eligible bachelors in the area walk in with a strange woman on
his arm. For his part, Jake hadn't missed the way some of
the younger women's eyes lingered on her speculatively, or
the way some of the older women elbowed their husbands
and nodded in her direction. A few minutes later those same
husbands would sidle over and, after the ritual of discuss-
ing weather and calf yields, would turn the conversation to
Dani and her relationship with "their" Jake.

"If another person asks me if I'm your cousin," Dani snapped after one too many of these assaults, "I'm going to scream!"

Jake glanced down at her. "I could always start introducing you as my wife, à la Claudia Schefer."

"And get me lynched? If looks could kill, I'd be dead ten times over as it is. Every woman of marriageable age in the Cariboo has her sights on you, cowboy. I'm definitely in the way here tonight."

Jake laughed quietly and slipped his arm around her shoulders, giving her a quick hug. "No, you're not, buttercup." She smiled, relaxing into the curve of his arm as though belonging there, and Jake let himself luxuriate in her nearness, refusing to let his earlier gloom spoil a perfect evening. For one evening he could pretend she was his. And when tomorrow came and the dream shattered...well, he'd handle that as he'd handled every disappointment in his life. And maybe, after enough time had passed, he'd be able to forget he'd even done the dreaming.

"There's Buster," Dani said suddenly.

His grandfather, comfortably installed in his wheelchair with pillows and blankets, was gesturing to them impatiently from one of the nearby rows of chairs. Most of people in the crowd were starting to edge their way to their seats, and Jake gave Buster an acknowledging wave. "It's going to start in a couple of minutes. We might as well sit down."

"Wondered where you two had gone off to," Buster grumbled as Jake and Dani took their seats. "My little girl okay?"

"All dressed up and raring to go," Jake assured him. "How about you? Is there anything you need before this thing starts?"

"I'm fine," Buster growled, waving him off. "Think I was a damn invalid the way people been hangin' around me all night!"

Smiling, Dani tucked the blanket around Buster's knees, making sure it covered the toes sticking out of the heavy cast on his right leg. "Are you sure you're okay?" she asked quietly.

Buster glowered at her, then shook his head a little sheepishly. "It's painin' me some. Suppose it wouldn't hurt none if I took another of these pills the doc gave me." He fumbled in the pocket of his robe and held out the bottle.

"I don't imagine it would." Dani very efficiently whipped the cap off the bottle and spilled two capsules into Buster's palm. "But for the heck of it, why don't you take the two the label recommends?" She unscrewed the cap from the thermos of water Jake had filled earlier and poured him a drink, then watched as Buster swallowed the two capsules without argument.

How the hell had she done *that*, Jake wondered. If he'd been the one to suggest his grandfather take two capsules, it would have precipitated a bellow of indignant protest. Whatever magic this woman spun, she spun it well!

Buster handed her the cup with a sly twinkle in his eyes. "Thank you, honey. You're a great little daughter-in-law." Dani cast Jake a startled look, and Buster laughed. "That Schefer woman was in to see me yesterday. Courtesy call, she said. But she was just snoopin' around, like always. Told her to get the hell out or I'd have the duty nurse *throw* her out."

Dani, whose cheeks had turned an intriguing shade of pink, looked at Buster worriedly. "I can explain ev—"

"No need to explain," Buster assured her. "I figured out what was goin' on. I might be old, but I ain't slow. Besides," he added with a sly look at Jake, "it wouldn't hurt my feelings none if it was to come true."

Or mine, Jake found himself thinking as he gazed down at Dani.

"Shh!" Buster suddenly said, leaning forward attentively. "Curtain's goin' up. Now where's that little gal of mine?"

If Beth Wilson's goal in producing *Heaven Loves Cowgirls* was to promote cooperation among her little theatrical group, she'd succeeded beyond anything Dani had anticipated. The half-hour play, even if it didn't always go according to the script, went off without a hitch. There were one or two tense moments. The first came when the leading lady, the cowgirl of the title, froze when the curtain went up and she found herself facing an expectant audience. The towheaded boy playing the pony gave her a nudge that nearly knocked her off her feet. He whispered a few lines to prompt her, and she blinked and picked up her role as smoothly as any Broadway actress. The second came a few minutes later when the lead troll missed his cue, and a golden-haired angel stepped forward and not only ad-libbed a few lines to keep the play moving, but whispered something in his ear that catapulted him stage center to deliver his part flawlessly.

That same golden-haired angel, whose costume sent murmurs of admiration throughout the audience, went on to play her part as though born to the stage. She had only a couple of brief setbacks, one when an elf who was supposed to exit stage left got confused and wandered forlornly around the set trying to find the way out. Then one of the blue-faced pansies in the chorus suddenly burst into tears and had to be comforted before the angel could get on with her role. All in all, it was a magnificent success.

The entire troupe got a standing ovation and was brought back for three curtain calls. Beth Wilson, beaming with pride, introduced each of the actors in turn, and when she came to Cassie, Buster had to be physically restrained from leaping to his feet, broken leg forgotten in the excitement.

"That's my great-granddaughter!" he proclaimed loudly to everyone within earshot. "That's my Cassie!"

"Did I do okay, Daddy?" Cassie asked, vibrating with energy when she got off the stage. Her cheeks were flushed and her eyes sparkled. "I didn't forget any of my lines or nothin'!"

"You were fantastic!" Jake laughed and swept her up in a bear hug that made her squeal. "But what did you say to Robby Jacobsen in Act One that lit such a fire under him?"

Cassie smiled angelically. "I just told him if he messed up I'd beat the stuffing out of him."

Dani nearly strangled trying not to laugh at the expression on Jake's face. "Well, from a bottom-line aspect," she told him with a grin, "you have to admit it was pretty effective."

Jake let Cassie slip to the floor, and she sped off through the crowd. Watching her, he shook his head. "I'm going to have to have a long talk with that kid." Then he looked down at his grandfather and grinned. "But first, old man, we've got to get you back up to the hospital before they send a posse out after us. Your two-hour parole was up about twenty minutes ago."

"Now I know how Cinderella felt when midnight hit," Buster grumbled. "Think I was goin' to turn into a pumpkin or somethin'!"

But he didn't argue when Dani started gathering up blankets and pillows, and she realized the evening had tired him more than he'd admit. With Beth Wilson's help they loaded him and his wheelchair into Beth's big car, then Dani joined Jake and an excited heavenly angel in Jake's pickup and they all went up to the hospital for a final good-night.

It was hours later when they got back to the ranch. Cassie was asleep in Dani's lap, wings a bit bent, halo tilted rakishly to one side, her mouth curved in a contented smile.

Jake laughed as he eased the sleeping child out of Dani's arms and carried her into the house. "To look at her you'd think butter wouldn't melt in her mouth."

"In a lot of ways," Dani replied with a soft laugh, "she takes after her father."

Grinning lazily, he glanced down at her. "Meaning?"

"Meaning," Dani said as she followed him up the stairs, "that the answer is no."

"What the hell was the question?" Jake looked sincerely puzzled as he nudged the door to Cassie's room open with his shoulder. He stood back and let Dani go in first.

As she stepped by him, Dani smiled tolerantly, not bothering to turn on the light. She tossed Cassie's dress and shoes onto a chair, then walked across and drew back the comforter and sheets on the small bed. "You told Buster you were going to ask me to stay a few more days."

Gently Jake placed his sleeping daughter on the bed. "You heard that, did you?"

"I did." Dani sat on the edge of the bed and started unbuttoning Cassie's angel costume. Behind her, Jake said nothing as he slipped Cassie's shoes off. Together, they eased her out of her costume and under the covers. Dani brushed a handful of fine blond hair off Cassie's cheek, then tucked the comforter under her chin. "She really is beautiful," she whispered, pausing for a moment to gaze down at the sleeping child. "You're very lucky, you know. When Darren and I divorced, I came out of it with nothing but a lot of anger and hurt, and a pile of bills and a credit rating so bad I couldn't charge a cup of coffee. Bad memories...that's all."

"It took me a long time to understand that," Jake said quietly. "Then one day I realized that having Cassie in my life was worth the hurt Sandra and I put each other through."

Dani nodded, then got up with a sigh and started hanging Cassie's clothes.

Jake stood up and stretched. He winced and flexed his left shoulder, rubbing it as he walked to the door. "That bottle of liniment still in the bathroom?"

"Downstairs." Dani closed the closet door and followed him out into the corridor. "Pulled muscle?"

"Pulled something," he muttered, flexing his shoulder. "I was piling fence posts this afternoon and felt something give." He gave her a sidelong glance as they walked downstairs together. "I don't suppose I could coax you into giving a saddle-sore, broken-down old cowboy a rubdown, could I?''

"If you can find me a saddle-sore, broken-down old cowboy, I might consider it," Dani retorted.

Jake grinned. "That wasn't a come-on."

"It sounded like a come-on."

"If I was planning on coming on to you, Dani Ross," he said in a husky purr, "I wouldn't waste my time concocting some line about pulled muscles and horse liniment."

His eyes held Dani's just long enough to make her heart give a thump. "Oh?"

"No." He paused in the bathroom door, looking down at her with a lazy smile. "I'd take you by the hand and lead you down to my bedroom. Which," he added in that husky voice, "is just down there. Then I'd peel you out of those pretty clothes until the only thing you'd be wearing would be that perfume that drives me crazy. After that I'd put you across my bed and—"

"I don't think I want to hear the rest!" Dani held her hand up, trying not to sound half as shaken as she felt. "I get the idea. And you're right. In comparison a pulled muscle and horse liniment isn't much of a come-on." It took every ounce of self-control she possessed, but Dani stepped by him and pulled open the medicine chest above the sink.

She found the bottle of liniment and reached up for it even as Jake's hand came from behind her and caught her wrist gently. He meshed his fingers with hers and drew her hand back, slipping his other arm around her waist, and Dani closed her eyes, not even breathing, as he started kissing the side of her throat.

Nine

——

"I'd kiss your throat, just like this," Jake whispered. "And your neck, your ear. I'd kiss you *here*, Dani." He cupped her breast, teasing the hardening nipple with his palm, then ran his hand slowly down her stomach. "And here. And here..." His hand brushed the juncture of her thighs. "And then I'd make love to you," he whispered. "For a long, long while, deep and slow and—"

"Jake, for the love of God!" It was all Dani could do to stand, knowing if he let go of her now she'd crumple like a rag doll. "It's not fair, driving me crazy like this when I—" *When I can't have you.* She took an unsteady breath. "We agreed it's insane to start something we can't finish, Jake. We agreed!"

"I know." He stood very still, his breath tickling the back of her neck. She could feel the tension in him, every muscle as taut as steel cable. "Everything used to be so simple," he whispered, running his lips lightly along her hairline. "It wasn't supposed to get this complicated, was it?"

"No." She managed a shaky laugh.

He stood motionless for a long while, just holding her, and Dani found herself not even breathing, waiting for him to say whatever was on his mind. It was like being poised on the edge of a precipice, waiting for the push that would send her tumbling over. But it never came.

He sighed finally, let his arms drop from around her and kissed the back of her neck lightly. "I can manage this liniment on my own. Why don't you go to bed and get some sleep?"

"All right." Very carefully, half expecting her legs to give out from under her, Dani stepped away. Not daring to look at him, she whispered, "Good night," and fled.

Jake stood there quite some time after she'd gone, trying to convince himself it was better this way. It *was* crazy to start something they couldn't finish. Hell, he knew that! One night with her would only make the rest of them even harder to get through. And it wouldn't be fair for her, either. She'd already admitted she'd wound up caring more than she'd expected to, probably more than she'd ever *wanted* to. It didn't take much insight to see how much she cared for Cassie and Buster, how caught up in their lives she'd become. She was going to carry enough of Silvercreek away with her without adding even more to her sense of loss. He didn't have the right to do that to her.

Restless, he prowled the quiet, dark house for nearly an hour before finally going to bed. And once in bed, he lay there listening to the distant hoot of a barn owl, knowing that sleep was going to be hard to come by tonight. As he'd been doing more and more frequently of late, he found himself thinking about his marriage to Caroline Wainwright.

The strange part of it was the lack of emotion he felt one way or the other. It was as though the marriage was going to happen to someone else, someone he didn't even know. How could he be marrying Caroline when the woman he *wanted* to marry was asleep upstairs right now?

Finally admitting it outright like that didn't make him feel any better. He swore under his breath and rolled onto his side, kicking off the blankets constricting him. Damn it, how had he gotten himself into this mess? Falling in love hadn't been part of this whole scheme. All he'd wanted was a wife—love had never come into it.

If it *was* love, he reminded himself with another burst of profanity. If he was brutally honest about it, he didn't know if what he was feeling was love or a bad case of simply wanting what he couldn't have. So it all came down to the same thing; Dani was going back to Toronto, and he was going to marry Caroline and everyone would live more or less happily ever after. End of story.

He gave his pillow a ferocious punch, then forced himself to close his eyes. *You just gotta live with it,* he could hear Buster telling him sagely. *There are some things you just gotta learn to live with.*

He had no idea how much later it was that he heard the catch on the door click. The moon had come up and his room was flooded with cold silver light and sharp-edged shadows, and for a moment he wondered if he might still be asleep. The door glided silently open, and he lay there watching it, telling himself it was just Cassie, shaken up by the residue of a nightmare and needing a comforting hug before returning to her own room.

But it wasn't Cassie.

Jake frowned and raised himself on one elbow, half expecting the figure to vanish into dream mist. "Dani?"

Her eyes were very wide and dark in the moonlight, but her expression was calm, almost serene. "I tried to stay away," she said very softly. "I really tried, Jake. But..." She shrugged. Then, very slowly, she pulled one end of the belt securing her light robe.

It dropped to the floor and her robe fell open and Jake caught his breath. She was naked under it, her body as perfect as he'd known it would be. Her breasts gleamed in the moonlight like fine silver, dark-tipped, casting sickles of shadow across her ribs. He could see the indented sweep of her waist, the flare of hip, the faint curvature of her stomach, all polished with moonlight. There was a gathering of shadow where her thighs met, tantalizing for the promise it held, then the bold sweep of long, taut thigh.

"My God, Dani..." he whispered as he slid from between the sheets.

Just the moonlit image of her had filled him with fire, and as he walked slowly across the room toward her, he knew the sight of him, naked and ready for her, affected her in the same way. He reached around and bolted the door. There was no need for either of them to say a thing. The vital awareness that they'd both been fighting all week blazed between them, hot and alive, and he basked in its heat.

Slowly he reached out and pushed the robe off her shoulders, letting his palms caress her lightly. He felt her shiver. The robe slipped to the floor, and she was naked in the moonlight, eyes smoky as she watched him look at her. He drew his hands slowly down her arms, and even as he watched, the dark tips of her breasts seemed to swell. He cupped his hands lightly around them, their smooth weight filling his palms. Then, murmuring her name, he moved his hands down to her waist and tugged her gently nearer, lowering his mouth to hers.

Her lips parted at his first touch, and she welcomed the probing thrust of his tongue with her own. Her mouth was wine-sweet and warm, and he felt himself getting drunk on her taste, each voluptuous swirl of her tongue against his a promise, each catch of her breath an entreaty. Her hands rested on his arms, then moved up to his shoulders, fingers of one hand slipping through his hair while the others curled around his neck. And then she stepped against him and the polished silver body was suddenly flesh, warm against his.

He had to struggle to catch his breath, heard her quick inhalation at his first explicit touch. She sighed with pleasure and arched her back. Jake felt his control slip dangerously. He slid his hands down the long sweep of her back to cup her bottom in his hands, lifting, pressing her against him. She sighed again and gave a sinuous wriggle cupping him fully between her thighs, and for an instant Jake nearly lost what tenuous grip he still had.

"It is really you, isn't it?" he groaned. "You're not just a dream, are you?"

"Do dreams do this?" she whispered, nipping his lower lip, tongue sliding, coaxing. "Or this?" Jake gritted his teeth as she drew her hand slowly down his chest and stomach, then lower still to touch him with gently questing fingers. "I don't care if this is wrong," she whispered. "All I want is this one night, Jake, I'll settle for that."

"You can have it all," he growled, kissing her hungrily. "You can have forever, Dani. All you have to do is reach out and take it."

"No." She put her fingertips across his mouth, her eyes searching his in the moonlight. "Please. No promises we can't keep, all right? I don't want to think about forever, or even about tomorrow. I just want tonight with you."

"Dani—"

"Make me happy, Jake," she said. "Make love to me the way you promised, deep and slow and—" The rest was lost as her mouth found his and she kissed him with an intensity that snapped his last bit of control.

He picked her up, carried her across to his bed and lowered her onto it, tossing the sheet and blankets aside impatiently. Kissing her feet and slender ankles, he slid slowly upward, tracing the inner curve of her knee with his tongue, then up the down-soft skin of her inner thigh.

He cupped her hips in his hands and moved that small, final distance to the warmth between, wild for her taste, hearing her gasp as he caressed her with his tongue. She was silk and fire and she shivered and whispered his name in a moan of pleasure. He drew his mouth from her slowly and ran a line of damp kisses up her stomach to her breasts, taking the soft, full peak of one, then the other into his mouth to savor.

Time, reality, lost all meaning. Nothing existed but the two of them, locked together in a moonlit room with only the sound of their whispered voices and their sighs of pleasure. He was wind and she was fire, he sweeping through her, touching her, marking her while she burned deep into the walls of his very soul. And he gave himself to her without hesitation.

And when he lay between her thighs, he cupped her face in his hands, eyes locked with hers, wanting to capture the moment forever. Her eyes widened as he slipped himself slowly into her welcoming warmth, and she bit her lip to stifle her soft moan, her fingers tightening on his shoulders.

Her gaze burned into his, filled with a thousand unspoken things, and he knew the closeness they were sharing at that moment exceeded mere physical intimacy, exceeded anything either of them had ever known before. He started to move slowly and deeply within her and watched the desire in her eyes turn to need.

Nothing was said beyond what he could read in her eyes and what he knew she could read in his. Slowly, he sensed the growing urgency within her, allowed himself to recognize the matching urgency within himself. Instinctively he echoed her quickening rhythm, pushing himself onto his forearms to deepen each thrust. Dani's eyes were closed now, and she slid her legs up to grip his hips. He could see the dark peaks of her breasts, moist where their sweat had mingled and felt the rhythmic flex of her fingers where she grasped his waist.

The muscles in her thighs tightened, the first tiny spasms starting within her, and he knew even before she did how near she was to the edge. Her fingers tightened, pulling him into her, and he responded with a deep thrust of his hips. Looking down, he found the sight of her responding to his lovemaking as erotic and satisfying as the lovemaking itself.

He felt the first wave sweep through her and paced his movements to heighten and prolong the crest. He was rewarded with a soft cry as she arched strongly against him as the crescendo built and built, then broke, spilling through her with rippling shivers that he felt as clearly as though they were his own.

Only then did he unclench his teeth and let his own body take what it needed. He relinquished what remained of his self-control as Dani smiled and responded with an erotic precision designed to drive him out of his mind. It very nearly succeeded, and at that last cataclysmic instant when the universe and everything in it exploded, he was conscious only of crying her name and of her voice answering.

Dawn finger-painted the sky. Dani lay warm and drowsy within the curve of Jake's body and watched the palette of colors shift and play across the east. The mountains had been purple velvet when she'd first opened her eyes, but now they were blushing, their peaks flaring molten gold with the rising sun.

She could hear Jake's deep breathing as he slept. His arms were still locked around her, his cheek resting against her hair, and she could feel the thump of his heart. It was strange, feeling so much a part of another person that she couldn't tell the beat of one heart from the other.

They had spent the entire night locked in each other's arms, talking softly, laughing, making love. Perhaps they'd slept, but she couldn't remember. There had been moments when she'd thought she had to be dreaming. Dani smiled sleepily. Her thighs ached, and the provocative tenderness between them was no dream. Both were as real as the man sleeping at her side, testament to a night she would never forget.

The birds were starting to sing now. A lone chickadee began its unmelodious chant, but its voice was all but drowned out by a distant blue jay's raucous cry. Dani sighed, know-

ing she couldn't postpone it. He'd be awake soon, and that
would only complicate things.

She slid from Jake's embrace and sat up, shivering as the
mountain air slipping through the open window curled
around her shoulders. Tugging the blanket around herself,
she sat there for a moment, willing herself to get up.

"You're up mighty early." A warm male hand settled
onto the flare of her hip.

Dani's heart sank. She glanced around. "Did I wake
you?"

"The draft woke me," he complained with a grin.

"Oh. Sorry." She tucked the sheet and blankets around
him again, holding one corner of the sheet around herself.

"I'd like it better if you were under here with me."

Dani didn't say anything, but simply stared out the window at the mountains. They were peach-colored now, the
sky above them the pale blue of skim milk.

"You're going to leave, aren't you?" His voice was quiet.
"Even now."

Especially now. "Yes. I . . . I've stayed too long already."

"Dani . . ."

"Please, Jake, don't make this harder than it already is."

"You can't leave. Not now. Not after last night." He sat
up and slipped his arms around her, kissing the sensitive
spot behind her ear. "You're part of me, Dani Ross. Part of
this ranch. Even part of those mountains out there. We're
all in your blood, just like I promised. You'll never be free
of us."

Dani pulled the sheet tighter around her shoulders, trying
to ignore the touch of his mouth, the warmth his body
promised. "I have to leave, Jake. I never meant it to . . . to
be forever."

His arms tightened. She heard him whisper an oath. "I
thought you didn't believe in one-night stands, buttercup.
Or am I an exception?"

"Damn it, Jake, don't you do this to me!" Dani leaped
out of the bed and crossed to where her satin robe still lay

puddled on the carpet. She slipped it on, shivering as she wrapped the icy fabric around herself. "You knew it was just last night."

"I'd *hoped* it was—"

"No!" Dani wheeled away from the window to glare down at him. "Don't play those games with me, Jake. We're not kids. We both know the facts of life. I came in here because it *was* just for one night—the last night. You knew that. Don't try to change all the rules this morning!"

"Games?" He stared across the room at her. "Rules? What the hell is this all about, Dani? This isn't some damn *game* we're playing here."

"I know that," she whispered, turning away again. Leaving was going to be like severing a part of herself. She'd known it was going to be difficult, but she'd never dreamed it would be like this....

She closed her eyes, praying she wasn't going to get maudlin and start crying. Not after all the promises she'd made to herself that she wouldn't! Last night, she'd told herself that one night with him was worth the pain, that she'd leave in the morning with a smile, regretting nothing, leaving nothing of herself behind, taking nothing but a few memories. How in God's name had she ever believed that was possible!

"Last night was—" she shook her head, searching for the right word "—something that comes along once in a million years, Jake. It was wonderful and special, something I'll treasure as long as I live, but..." She shrugged helplessly, not even knowing what she was trying to say.

Jake sat looking at her, filled with a desperate yearning he only half understood. He wanted her to stay, would say whatever it took to *make* her stay—and yet, deep down, he knew he was just kidding himself. He'd never really believed it would last. Even last night, buried so deep in her they were one breath, one pulse, one soul, he'd never truly believed it. Hadn't *dared* to believe it. But now—in the cold,

hard light of dawn—it hurt more than he'd ever anticipated.

He left the bed and walked across to where she was
standing, still so warm from her he scarcely felt the cold. He
reached out to touch her, but held back, palms only inches
from the blue satin of her robe. "Whatever last night was,
buttercup," he said softly, "it *was* real."

"Was it?" She turned to look at him, eyes dark in the
dawn light. They held his, searching for heaven knows what.
"Or did we just want it to be real? Just for a little while?"

He knew exactly what she meant, but at the moment, still
filled with the taste and feel of her, he didn't want to think
about it. "Does it matter?"

"Of course it matters!" She frowned and turned away
again. "Or maybe it doesn't. I don't know. I don't know
anything anymore except that I—" She stopped, shoulders
rigid, staring out across the hills as though those distant
mountains held some secret she needed to know.

Except that you what? He stared at that stiff little back,
willing her to turn around, to say... what? That she was as
confused as he was by what was happening between them?
That it had caught her by surprise as much as it had caught
him, and that she wasn't too certain how to handle it?

Jake's stomach had turned itself into a tight, hard knot.
He put his hand slightly on her shoulders, half afraid to
touch her in case she vanished into the morning like the
afterglow of a dream. "I want you to stay." It was easier
than he'd anticipated, but he exhaled with some difficulty.
"Dani—"

"No." She shook her head abruptly. "You're asking too
much, Jake. I ... I can't have an easy short-term affair with
you and then go back to Toronto as though nothing's
changed."

"I didn't say anything about an easy short-term affair,"
he said through his teeth, not knowing what he *had* meant.

"What else could it be?" She pulled away from his grasp angrily. "You're not mine to have, Jake. You're Caroline's."

"Damn Caroline!" he retorted just as angrily, his sense of desperation, of loss, growing by the minute. "Tear that contract up if that's what's bothering you. I don't want Caroline. I want you. And you don't have to go back to Toronto. You can stay here. You can stay for as long as you want." He hadn't even known he was going to say the words until they were out, had listened to them with the same surprise with which Dani was looking at him now.

Her eyes were very bright, abnormally bright, and it took him a moment to realize they were filled with unshed tears. It surprised him so much that he simply stared back, as confused and uneasy at the sight of her tears as he was by any woman's. He never knew how to respond—how they *wanted* him to respond—and it was no different now.

"You don't mean that," she whispered.

"Dani..." Damn it, what *did* he mean? He found it impossible to think clearly with those eyes locked on his, with her taste still honey-sweet in his mouth. Something had pulled so tight within him that he could hardly breathe, and he wanted nothing more at that moment than to pull her back across that rumpled bed and lose himself in her.

"It's like playing with fire, Jake," she said after a moment, giving an abrupt laugh that sounded more like a sob. "You can keep it at arm's length and it'll warm you, but if you get too close, it'll burn you to the bone. If I stay, we'll both get burned. Don't you see that? We'll wind up breaking all the rules we've set, and we'll get hurt all over again."

"It doesn't have to be like that," he said tightly.

"But it is!" She squeezed her eyes shut and wheeled away from him, as though she'd be damned if she'd let him see her cry. "One of us will ruin it all by falling in love or something stupid! And you know as well as I do that love doesn't work. It's a lie, just like the lie that brings a moth too near the flame. It gets hypnotized by the promise of something it doesn't even understand, and it gets burned!''

He looked down at her, thinking fleetingly of Sandra. Of Dani's ex-husband. Of all the promises and all the tears. Of fires that had burned too deeply. But they were fire-hardened, too. Sword makers heated steel blue-white, and from that tempering came durability, came flexibility. Came strength.

And love? Where in hell did *love* fit into this puzzle? She'd called it a lie, but he was starting to wonder if it was love that was the lie, or just the illusions that surrounded it. Perhaps if one managed to sweep away those illusions what was left was pure truth. Pure love. Perhaps...

He shook his head, scattering the thoughts. It was too early in the day to work out complexities he only partly understood in the first place. He reached toward her, somehow sensing that if he could hold her, if he could make her stay, that it would all unravel and become clear in time.

"I'm sorry, Jake," she said quietly, walking to the door without even looking back. "It's better this way. S-say goodbye to Buster for me, will you? And Cassie. Tell her I was proud of her last night and that I—Just tell her goodbye!''

She slipped through the door like a wraith and was gone. Jake watched the door swing closed and suddenly realized he was chilled to the bone. The breeze blowing through the window carried the ice of the high mountains, and he started pulling on his clothes with a quiet, heartfelt oath. It was already too late to worry about being burned, he told himself ferociously. The only question was, which of them had been the moth, and which the flame?

"Dani, are you working here or just taking up office space?" Carla Santos strode across Dani's office, a stack of files in her hands. She threw herself into the plush chair across from Dani and tossed the files onto the desk. "You left these on my desk two days ago—and they're current work by the look of it." She shook her head despairingly. "I don't know about you, kid. If you weren't a good friend as well as a sister-in-arms in this madhouse, I'd be trying to get you replaced."

Dani leaned back in her chair and rubbed her forehead with her fingers. "I've been meaning to pick them up all day."

"What's going on, Dani? I've been juggling accounts like crazy for the past two weeks to give you time to get back into full gear after that Wainwright thing. But I can't hold on much longer. You've got a backlog of appointments right into next week, and your secretary says you've been sitting in here like a zombie for days, just staring out the window."

Guilt shot through Dani. She stared at her pen, toying with it, wishing she had either the energy or even the interest to defend herself. "I know. I'm sorry."

"Damn it, Dani, I *know* you're sorry! That's not the point." Carla stood up impatiently and paced back and forth. "I thought at first that you were just tired, that after a few days you'd be up to speed. But you're not even here half the time! Oh, your body's here, all right, but your mind is somewhere out *there*." She gestured toward the windows.

"You won't go out with us for a drink after work, you skip lunch, you drag yourself in here every morning looking as though you've gotten no sleep. And you won't talk about it." She stood in front of the desk, hands on hips.

Dani forced herself to smile. "I'm fine, Carla. Really. It's just a bug I picked up."

"Bug, my foot," Carla snapped. "It was a man, wasn't it?"

Dani's gaze strayed to the window, as it did so many times during the day. West. Always she found herself looking west.... She shook herself free of the reverie and looked at Carla. "Do you ever get up in the morning, look around and feel like walking out? Just leaving it all behind?"

"Every morning. Then I have a large cup of coffee and a glance through my charge account bills, and suddenly everything's fine again." Carla sighed. "Dani, you didn't get to be one of ManHunters' finest by getting up every morning wondering whether to come into work or not. What happened out there? According to Marion Wainwright-Syms, you were staying on that ranch as part of your interview with the owner. But I don't think Marion knows the half of it."

Dani smiled very faintly. Thank goodness Marion *didn't* know the half of it! She realized Carla was still looking at her speculatively and she shrugged. "When I moved to Toronto, I never thought I'd ever want to go back to the prairies. This city was like Disneyland to a kid right off the farm! But when I was out on that ranch..." She frowned and shrugged again. "I can't even explain it. There was something about the air, the way the wind smelled of trees and mountains. I realized I missed seeing cattle grazing on a hillside, the horse-and-leather smell of a stable on a cold morning."

"If you're homesick for the smell of horses and leather," Carla said dryly, "I'll pick up a bottle of men's cologne and we'll just sprinkle some around your office."

Dani laughed. "I wish it were that simple." She tossed the pen aside and sighed deeply. "Oh, I don't know, Carla! Part of it was facing my roots, I guess. And part of it was seeing people do a hard day's work—sweat-raising, physical labor—and getting something worthwhile accomplished."

"You mean like punching cows?" Carla arched an elegant eyebrow.

"Yes, like punching cows," Dani said with another laugh. "I watched three men spend an entire day on horseback, moving more than four hundred head of cattle from the lower pastures up to their summer grazing. It was hot, hard work, and they came in that night exhausted, but they'd done something *real*, Carla. Something that mattered. And I met this marvelous woman, a retired schoolteacher who got tired of spending her days gardening and started an afternoon activities group for isolated preschoolers. She's got all those half-wild little kids creating *plays*, for God's sake—not just writing, but making the sets and doing the acting."

"And you don't think recruiting manpower for some of the biggest corporations in the world is real work?"

Dani looked squarely at Carla. "I used to think I was doing something important and worthwhile. But since I've been back, Carla, all I see are a bunch of spoiled, overpaid executives who want it all. They've got no goals, aside from making a lot of money and getting to the president's office as quickly as possible. No loyalty—highest bidder takes all. I'm not a career planner. I'm an agent. I negotiate for the best terms, that's all.

"Company A wants an employee who's now working for Company B, so I go in and present their offer. He comes back with a counteroffer. We dicker a bit, fine-tune it. If he moves to Company A, I get a fat commission. If I'm really good, I can get a bidding war going between the two companies, so I get a commission regardless of *which* way he goes. And in the end it means nothing, Carla, just a lot of high-priced kids playing power games."

Carla gave a low, tuneless whistle. "I've seen it happen before, Dani, but I honestly didn't think I'd live long enough to see *you* burn out."

"You think that's what it is?"

"I know that's what it is. You've been here—what? Five years? Six? The pressure alone gets most people in the first eight months. You're some kind of a legend as it is."

Dani looked at her. "So now what?"

Carla shrugged. "Quit. Find something else. Hardly a week goes by that you don't get a job offer from some big company. Pick out the best. Take a few weeks off, maybe. Relax." She smiled. "Find the sparkle again, Dani. You've just been pushing it too hard for too long."

"Maybe you're right." Dani sighed again and glanced at the window. West. Always west . . .

"You're not thinking of moving back to Saskatchewan or wherever you're from, are you?" Carla drawled. "Although, if you do, remember I have dibs on your apartment."

Dani had to laugh. Toronto's rental situation was the worst in Canada at the moment, and even friendship was no match for a rent-controlled apartment in a good neighborhood. "Sorry, Carla, but I'm not planning on moving back to Saskatchewan."

Carla shrugged philosophically. "But you *are* coming to my party tonight."

Dani stifled a groan. She'd forgotten all about it. And, for one rash moment, she was tempted to beg off. But one glance at Carla's expression convinced her otherwise, and she managed a weak smile. "Wouldn't miss it."

"Liar," Carla told her cheerfully. She turned and started for the door. "Eight sharp. And with bells on. I've invited three men for every woman, just to keep things interesting." She paused at the door and looked around with a wicked smile. "Because what *you* need, Dani Ross, is a man in your life!"

A man, Dani thought disconsolately a few hours later, was about the last thing she needed right now. She assessed her reflection in the big mirror above her bathroom vanity, then turned away and switched off the light. She'd spent nearly an hour getting ready for Carla's party, hoping that the very act of putting on pretty clothes and makeup would generate some enthusiasm. But she felt no more like going now than she had that afternoon.

But there was no getting around it. Burned out or not, if she didn't put in an appearance at Carla's tonight, she'd suffer the consequences. She didn't have to stay—an hour at the most. A glass of wine, a few minutes of party small talk, then she could leave, inventing a sudden headache if need be.

She wandered through her living room, adjusted a throw pillow and fussed with an arrangement of flowers that was already perfect. Standing in front of the big window overlooking the city, she stared out at the twinkling lights. They filled her view, a wonderland of tinsel and fireflies. But she was seeing mountains. And a tall, wide-shouldered man with a devil's grin and outlaw eyes....

She turned away from the window and wandered around the room restlessly, stopping finally to yank the flowers out of the vase, heedless of the dripping water. One by one she started putting them back, then finally just jammed the entire bunch back into the vase, not caring what they looked like. Maybe Carla was right. Maybe she should take a few weeks off. Just get in the car and drive. East, maybe. Nova Scotia. South to Bar Harbor, Boston, Cape Cod. Sun, sand and sea. Wasn't that the classic prescription for a lovesick heart?

She glanced at her watch, then sighed and picked up her handbag and coat. In the meantime she might as well get Carla's party over with.

She was halfway across the spacious atrium lobby of her apartment building when she heard the commotion. It was coming from the desk near the entrance where the concierge sat watching his security monitors, but she didn't bother walking around to see what it was. Her high heels clicked sharply on the polished marble floor as she walked by the fountain in the center of the lobby, heading for the elevators that led down to the parking levels.

Two elegant women and their husbands were standing by the fountain, dressed in formal evening attire and obviously waiting for their car to be brought up. One of the men nodded at Dani, and she smiled back. She had no idea who he was, although he and his wife had been living in her building nearly as long as she had.

That was one thing she'd never quite gotten used to about living in the city; you could pass someone on the street daily for years and never get beyond the polite smiles of recognition. For some reason she found herself thinking about the Cariboo and how, in the short span of a few days, she'd felt part of a community again.

There was another angry exchange at the front desk, and she glanced in that direction, not even slowing her pace. It took her two full strides to realize what she was seeing, and she stopped so abruptly that a man behind her had to stumble aside to avoid running into her. He muttered something under his breath, but Dani hardly noticed him.

It was another man who held her full attention, the one arguing vehemently with the concierge, the tall, wide-shouldered one outfitted like a refugee from the rodeo circuit in jeans and sheepskin jacket, wide-brimmed Stetson and riding boots. The one who was advising the concierge in even, dangerous tones that unless he wanted a serious injury he'd better call Dani Ross's apartment again and tell her that Jake Montana was in the lobby and that he, by God, wasn't going anywhere without seeing her.

Ten
___

Jake saw her before the concierge did. His angry blue eyes gentled, then crinkled at the corners as he smiled that beguiling smile that always made her lose her breath. This time it not only made her breath catch; it took it completely away. She stared at him in astonishment, wondering if hallucinations were a normal part of career burnout.

But unless this particular hallucination was a group effort, the expression on the concierge's face made it clear that Jake was very real. She blinked and heard herself say, "Looking for me, cowboy?"

Jake's grin broadened. "All my life, buttercup."

It was so corny that she held her breath, half expecting someone to leap from behind the palms shouting, "Cut!" But no one did, and after a dazed moment or two she realized that the concierge and the four partygoers were watching them, obviously as curious about what was going to happen next as she was.

Jake's gaze suddenly swept her from head to foot, taking in the black crepe evening pants and spangled top she was wearing under her open coat, the elegant patent leather shoes with their three-inch heels and rhinestone bows. Something tightened around his eyes. "I guess I should have called from the airport."

"I did have plans..." Dani began uncertainly.

"With anyone special?"

He asked it with such unapologetic bluntness that Dani blinked. "I...no. No one special."

He nodded once, satisfied. Then he glanced around the lobby. "Is there somewhere we can talk? It won't take long."

Dani swallowed, her throat suddenly dry. "My apartment."

His gaze swung around and hit her face like a laser. "And your plans? Must be pretty fancy, judging by the getup you're wearing."

"Nothing I can't cancel."

He looked at her for a moment longer, as though weighing her words, then bent down to pick up the small canvas-and-leather satchel next to his feet.

"Miss Ross, would you like me to call security?" The concierge gave Jake a scathing look. "Or the police?"

"Thank you, William, but Mr. Montana and I are old friends."

William's eyebrows arched, but he restrained himself, even managing a pained smile. "I...see."

She and Jake walked to the elevators in silence, the tension between them as taut as wire. There was an elevator waiting, and they stepped in. Dani pushed her floor button and swallowed again, staring at the floor as the doors closed and the elevator rushed upward. She dared a sidelong glance at Jake, but he was staring at the indicator lights above the door.

The fleece collar on his sheepskin jacket was turned up, and he'd pulled his hat brim low so that all she could see was his eyes, thoughtful and introspective, not giving a clue about what was ticking behind them. He seemed even taller and more broad-shouldered here in the copper and smoked-glass elegance of the elevator, his rugged masculinity heightened by the delicacy of his surroundings. He reminded her of something powerful and wild, and she kept thinking of mountain lions, wondering if their prey ever heard the whisper of padded footfalls before the killing strike.

The elevator stopped, and she shook herself free of the mental image as the doors slid noiselessly open. She walked down the carpeted corridor toward her apartment, sensing more than hearing Jake following silently behind her. She stabbed her key into the lock and opened the door.

She'd left a lamp on in the living room, so she walked through the small entranceway toward it, suddenly wanting to get this reunion over as quickly as possible. "It's about Caroline Wainwright, isn't it?" she asked calmly over her shoulder. "You've changed your mind about marrying her."

She turned to face him when she reached the center of her living room, feeling slightly more in control now that she was on familiar ground.

He dropped the satchel and looked around him, his eyes sweeping the room. "Nice." His gaze brushed her face, then moved restlessly to the bookcases lining one wall.

"Thank you. Can I get you something? Coffee? A drink?"

"No." He perused the titles for a moment, then looked at her again. He was grim now, determined. "You're half right. I'm not going to marry Caroline. But that's not why I'm here."

"I should be furious." She gave her head an impatient shake, walked to the window and stared down at the bright, glittering lights. "But I've been half expecting it all along. I never did feel your heart was in it."

"My heart wasn't supposed to be in it, remember?" he shot back with a flash of dry humor. "I thought that was the whole point—a loveless love match, just common sense and cold logic.''

''You know what I mean.''

''I know what you mean.'' He looked at her, his eyes seeming to search hers for something he needed to know. Then, slowly, he started walking toward her.

Dani's heart gave a leap. Instinct told her to run, but she just stood there like a rabbit caught in the headlights. He moved silently on the thick carpet, very large and solid in the dimly lit room, and as he neared, she threw her hands up involuntarily to fend him off.

He smiled down at her, eyes lazy and warm. ''Scared?''

''No.'' Her voice was no more than a squeak.

His smile widened. ''You should be. I'm scared to death myself.''

''You are?'' Again she merely whispered.

''You love me, don't you?''

It occurred to her, vaguely, that she should be used to these abrupt turns of conversation, that he shouldn't be able to take her as completely off balance as he invariably did.

''It took me nearly two damn weeks to figure it out,'' he continued conversationally. ''It was staring me right in the face, but for the life of me I couldn't figure out why you'd bolted on me just when things were starting to fall into place. That business-client excuse didn't ring true, so I told myself you'd just been having a springtime romp like any filly cooped up over the winter.

''But that didn't make any sense, either. If that's all you'd been after, we'd have been together right from that first night. So I had to ask myself why a woman would come into a man's bed on her last night under his roof. Why—after it had been so good for both of them—she'd take off the next morning like a rope-shy yearling at the first sight of a saddle.''

Dani hadn't moved. *Couldn't* move. Her heart was hammering so loud that it was impossible for him not to hear it, and although she knew she ought to be saying something, her mind simply refused to work. He moved nearer, stepping through the barricade of her hands effortlessly, and she felt him cup her face, watched his face drop toward hers through a daze.

"Then I finally understood what it was that sent you running out of my life, Dani Ross," he murmured, his breath warming her mouth. His lips almost touched hers, pausing tantalizingly. "You broke all the rules and fell in love with me, didn't you? You came looking for your Ideal Man, and you found him. But you found a little more than you bargained for, right?"

His mouth brushed hers, and Dani felt herself lose all sense of reality, knew she should be pulling away. Was this all he'd come here for, to taunt her for doing what she'd sworn she'd never do? To pick up their relationship for a few days or weeks on *his* terms before going back to Silvercreek and putting her entirely out of his mind? The tip of his tongue moistened her lips, probed between them, silky and wet. Helplessly she touched it with her own, his taste so achingly familiar that she felt her body respond before willpower could intervene.

"Say it, Dani," he urged in a gritty whisper. "I want to hear you say it."

"Jake..."

"Say it," he breathed, catching her lower lip between his and sucking it gently before pulling back. "Say it."

"I love you," she whispered helplessly, feeling her coat slip off her shoulders and land in a heap at her feet. "I love you." She caught his marauding tongue as it glided between her lips again and drew it into her mouth. And then his mouth was on hers, hard and insistent, and the thrust of his tongue against hers wasn't playful anymore. His kiss was the deep, hungry kiss of a man who knew his woman and what she wanted, who knew what was his for the taking.

It was madness, sheer and simple, yet Dani didn't even try to fight it. She knew deep in her heart that she'd give whatever he wanted and give it willingly, wishing only that she had more to give. She didn't know if he had shucked her out of the sequined blouse, or if she'd slipped it off herself, didn't remember who had unfastened her evening pants, yet she stood in only her teddy a moment later The buttons of his shirt parted under her fingers, and she slid her hands along his ribs, up his shoulders, then down to his oval belt buckle.

He drew his stomach in, and she worked the buckle free, loosened the metal snap under it, then jerked the balky zipper down impatiently. He groaned at the first touch of her hand, whispering something in a thick voice. She started to draw her hand away, but he caught it in his and pressed it hard against himself.

His hands were on her, seeking and coaxing and wild, and then even the teddy slipped to the floor and she was naked, shivering in delight as his caresses grew more demanding. She thought of drawing her mouth from his long enough to tell him where the bedroom was, but she hesitated too long and then it was too late. All she wanted was to make love with him here and now, to be so filled with his taste and touch that he'd be imprinted on her soul.

The carpet was like moss under her, and she slipped her arms around Jake's shoulders, dimly realizing he was still wearing his shirt and sheepskin jacket. His remaining clothes fell open around her, cocooning her in the heat of his body, and then he was *there*, slipping so swiftly and deeply into her that she gave a startled gasp of satisfaction.

He groaned deeply, and then he was moving with strong, sure thrusts of his hips, obviously knowing that she was well past the point of needing slow preliminaries. Her body responded instantly, and she moved with him, thighs gripping his, feeling the cold bite of his belt buckle against her hip, knowing she was going to bruise but not caring. All that mattered was the bright, aching tension centering within her with astonishing swiftness, the urgency in Jake's powerful movements, the reality of having him there locked within her arms and body.

She heard her own voice lifting, soft, little breathless cries that seemed to drive Jake half-wild. He murmured her name, his mouth plundering hers in a deep kiss. She tried to catch the uprush before it got away from her, wanting it to last forever, but Jake must have sensed it within her because he suddenly rocked up on his knees, lifting her with him so that she was straddling him.

He wrapped his arms around her and lifted his hips sharply, then again, and Dani gave a soft cry as the tension within her exploded, then exploded again with a burst of such exquisite pleasure that she arched in his arms. He moved under her, setting off a chain of aftershocks she would have thought impossible. And even as she was struggling to catch her breath, she heard his sharp inhalation, then his muted shout of pure satisfaction.

His hair was damp with sweat, and she ran her fingers through it, kissing him. Arms locked around her, and she felt his heart stampeding against hers. He was panting as he kissed her throat and neck, cupped her head in both hands and nuzzled under her chin.

"How come," he murmured, "you're naked and I'm mostly not?"

"You were in more of a hurry than I was, I guess," she teased softly.

"God, I can't believe this!" he said, laughing huskily. "All the way out here I was telling myself I'd handle this like one of your city guys, cool and laid-back. And what happens? Ten minutes after getting here I'm tearing your clothes off and throwing you down on the rug like a cowhand just off a three-month cattle drive."

"And I loved it, cowboy," she whispered. "But there is *one* thing . . ."

"Name it."

"Your belt buckle's killing me."

Jake swore as he extricated the silver buckle from under her thigh. It had left an indentation in her soft skin, and he gently rubbed the bruised spot with his fingers. "Sorry, buttercup. You're going to have a mark there for a few days.''

"It doesn't matter," she murmured as she kissed him. "No one's going to see it but you." Her lips teased his. "But do you always brand your women?"

"Only the ones I intend to keep." She drew back to look at him, eyes dark and full of questions. Jake smiled as he eased her off him. He got to his feet stiffly, pulling up his jeans, then slipped off his heavy fleece-lined jacket and wrapped it around her.

Raking his fingers through his tangled hair, he sat on the edge of a nearby chair, forearms on thighs, and stared at the floor between his feet. "I'm not really good with words, Dani," he finally admitted softly. "I guess I was raised to believe a real man doesn't talk about his feelings, that we're supposed to keep everything bottled up inside even if it hurts." He looked up then and saw Dani still kneeling on the floor, watching him, jacket pulled tight around her. "But I've been hurting since you left, Dani. Hurting like hell. The morning you left you said love is like fire, that if you get too close you get burned. Well, I'm burning, buttercup. Burning deep. And the funny thing is, it feels good! It makes me feel alive, Dani. And do you know how long it's been since I've felt that way, since I haven't been just numb and dead inside?''

"Jake..."

He shook his head, stopping her, needing to get it all said. "After Sandra left, I convinced myself that love was just a game you played until you lost, a game I never intended to play again. Just like you did after you and Darren broke up, then again after you watched your parents split up. We both convinced ourselves that the answer to never feeling hurt again was just to never feel *anything* again. But, hell, Dani, you might as well be dead as go through life that way. You made me see that, because you reached inside me and touched places where I've never been touched before.''

She was sitting very still, his big jacket making her appear even smaller and more delicate than she was. She looked, Jake realized with an inward smile, scared to death. That wasn't surprising. He'd been plenty scared himself at first. He'd had a couple of weeks to get used to what she was hearing for the first time, a couple of weeks to worry it through and know there was no other answer.

"When you asked me if I'd come out here to tell you I wasn't marrying Caroline, I said you were half right. The other reason I came out here is to tell you . . . I love you."

He distinctly heard her suck in her breath, saw her eyes widen, and he had to laugh. "I know—it hit me like that, too, at first. It's kind of funny in a way, two cynics like us breaking all the rules and falling in love. We knew we were playing with fire, Dani—yet we couldn't keep our hands off each other. I think both of us knew what was happening right from that first day, but we'd promised ourselves and each other that we weren't going to do something stupid like falling in love. So we fought it. And each other."

He smiled. "But I'm tired of fighting it. I realize now that love doesn't come with any guarantees. You just have to take a deep breath, jump in and pray you can tread water long enough to learn to swim. I love you. I want to marry you. It's that simple."

"Simple." The word was no more than a whisper. "You were supposed to be the strong one, damn it," she said, swallowing hard. "You promised we wouldn't do anything stupid."

He grinned lazily at her. "I lied."

"And Caroline?"

Some of the color was starting to come back into her cheeks, and Jake smiled patiently, understanding her need to fight it to the bitter end. But he could wait. For this woman he could wait until the end of time itself if he had to. "Marrying Caroline was the answer back when I thought I'd never be able to love again—didn't *want* to ever love again. But marrying a woman I don't love would be settling for second best now, Dani, and I won't do that when I know I can have the real thing. There's only one woman I'm going to marry—and that's you."

"Oh, Jake." She closed her eyes, going so pale again that Jake thought for a moment or two that she was going to faint.

He got out of the chair and knelt in front of her, tucking the fleecy collar up around her ears. "I want you to come back to Silvercreek with me. You don't have to promise me anything. If you're scared of marrying me, just come out and live with me for as long as you're happy, no strings attached."

She drew in a deep, unsteady breath and looked up into his eyes. "You . . . you'd accept me on those terms?" she whispered incredulously.

"I love you," he told her quietly. "I'll take you on whatever terms you want. All I need is time." He smiled down at her. "You've already admitted you love me. All I have to do is wait until you finally realize there's nothing to be afraid of. And I can wait as long as it takes, buttercup. As long as you need."

"Oh, Jake, what have we done?" But she was laughing as she said it. Her eyes suddenly welled with tears, and a moment later she was in his arms, half sobbing and half laughing, her face buried in his neck. "I can't believe we've gone and fallen in love. Of all the stupid things to do!"

"It wasn't exactly on my agenda, either," he reminded her with a gentle laugh. "I suppose we're going to have to tell Caroline. And her sister."

"Oh, heavens," Dani groaned. "Poor Caroline! What am I going to tell her?"

"The truth. That you searched the entire Dominion of Canada for the Ideal Man—and found him."

"And I'm keeping him all to myself," she added with a mischievous chuckle. "I ought to be ashamed of myself. This isn't exactly ethical."

"That's life." Jake slipped his hands under the jacket. She was warm and soft, and he felt the gentle stirrings of desire that had only been briefly quenched. He nuzzled the collar aside to kiss her throat as he slid his hands around her ribs. "Do you have a bedroom in this place?"

"I have a bedroom," she whispered, her hands slipping under his open shirt, pulling it off. "Are you thinking what I'm thinking?"

"I certainly hope so," Jake murmured, the gentle stirrings definitely coming to life now. "I was thinking of crawling into bed with you and, among other things, having a closer look at this brand…." He slipped his hand along her thigh, watching her as he moved his hand upward a bit. Her eyes closed, and he felt her stiffen very slightly, heard her gasp.

"I think I'd like that, cowboy," she murmured. "I think I'd like that a lot."

Dani didn't know if it was the shrill summons of the telephone that woke her up, or the hammering on her apartment door. She lay there for a bleary moment or two trying to figure out what was happening, then got out of bed and pulled on her robe. Jake mumbled something in his sleep and rolled onto his back, covers kicked off, looking very large and rugged and unmistakably male against the delicate floral pastels of the sheets. It was a shock seeing him there in broad daylight, and Dani had to blink a couple of times to assure herself that he was real.

The telephone was still ringing insistently, and the pounding on her door was becoming rapidly more frantic. She swore at whoever was intruding into an otherwise idyllic morning, then staggered out into the living room and grabbed the telephone receiver even as she shouted for whoever was at the door to wait a minute.

It was the concierge on the phone, and he sounded desperate. "Said they were friends of yours and just barged right through, Miss Ross. Should I send security up?"

Dani blinked, still half asleep. "Nev'mind," she slurred. "Hafta go. Someone at the door." She hung up and was almost at the door before she figured out that whoever was out there trying to hammer it down was the same person the concierge had been calling about. She peered through the peephole and was startled to see Caroline Wainwright.

The sight of Caroline jolted her awake enough that by the time she had the door open she almost remembered who was still in her bed. "Oh, my God!" she exclaimed, staring at Caroline in horror.

But Caroline hardly seemed to notice. She brushed by Dani without a word, the young bearded man who was with her managing to give Dani an apologetic smile before Caroline wrenched him in by the arm. "Is my sister here?"

"Marion?" It was an inane question, considering Caroline only had one sister, and Dani shook herself. "It's seven-thirty on a Saturday morning, Caroline. I imagine she's home in bed." *Where you should be,* she nearly added. *Where I'd like to be....*

Caroline drew herself up to her full five feet two inches. "Dani, I'm sorry for coming over here without calling first, but this has gone on long enough! It never occurred to me that you might actually find someone that Marion would approve of, and even if you did, I never dreamed she'd really expect me to go through with it. Am I making any sense?" She stopped and peered worriedly at Dani, her eyes owl-like behind her glasses.

"No," Dani said calmly, deciding the whole world had gone a little mad. First Jake, now Caroline. "But that's all right. I rarely understand what people are talking about this early in the morning. Would you like some coffee?" She smiled at the man standing quietly to one side. "Tea?"

He gazed back at her speechlessly, and Caroline, blushing a furious shade of scarlet, slipped her arm through his and looked at Dani with touching defiance. "This," she said proudly, "is Jacob. We're getting married."

Dani simply stared at her. Then she drew in a deep breath and closed her eyes, rubbing the tight spot between her eyes. "Would either of you mind if *I* had a cup of coffee?"

Some of Caroline's bravado seemed to give way. She looked at Dani miserably. "You have every right to be angry with me, Dani. You spent months finding this Wyoming person for me and—"

"Montana," Dani corrected, sighing.

"—I wouldn't blame you if you sued me or something, but I couldn't get Marion to listen to me. You know what she's like! Every time I tried to tell her about Jacob she just waved her hands and told me not to be ridiculous, that I couldn't possibly be in love with an assistant professor of ancient languages. I think it's the *assistant* part she couldn't handle, although it could be because Jacob's father sells used cars in—"

"Please." Dani held up her hand to stem the barrage. "Be patient with me, Caroline. I was sound asleep until three minutes ago and I'm having a little trouble keeping up."

"Sorry," Caroline muttered. She stepped nearer to Jacob, who put his arm around her shoulders reassuringly. "It's just that when I called Marion last night to tell her I wouldn't be home, she had an absolute fit. And when I called back this morning, Cora, our maid, told me that Marion said that she figured that I'd come here sooner or later, so she was coming over herself—Marion, that is, not Cora—but I wanted—"

"Wait!" Dani threw her hand up again. She was beginning to feel as if she'd been hit by a very large truck. "You weren't home last night?"

Another blush spilled across Caroline's pale cheeks. "I stayed at Jacob's," she whispered, not meeting Dani's eyes.

"And Marion," Dani added unnecessarily, "was not pleased."

"We shouldn't have broken it to her like that," Jacob admitted quietly. "We should have gone over there and faced her squarely instead of sneaking around."

"I was the one who convinced Jacob that I should call Marion from his place," Caroline whispered. "And I was scared to do even that. I was sure she'd track his address down through the university and arrive on the doorstep with the police to arrest Jacob for...for kidnapping or something."

"And so you thought—" Dani stopped. "Did you say she was coming *here*?"

Caroline nodded. "That's what Cora said. That's why Jacob and I came right over. I wanted to talk with you before—"

The intercom buzzed, cutting her off, and a second later there was a pounding on Dani's apartment door only slightly more urgent than before. Caroline and Jacob traded nervous glances. Dani groaned and reached for the intercom receiver. "It's all right, William. She's a friend."

"Miss Ross," the concierge said crisply, "I think it would be more productive all around if you'd suggest to your guests that they use the—"

"I'll do that, William, thanks." Dani cut him off in midprotest, walked to the door and pulled it open. "Come in, Marion. Could I get *you* a cup of coffee? I have a feeling this is going to be a long morning."

"I didn't call before coming over," Marion Wainwright-Syms announced as she strode past Dani, "because I wasn't certain you'd tell me the truth if what I *suspect* has happened has happened. That sister of mine has—well, you *are* here!"

"Dani didn't know what was going on until a couple of minutes ago," Caroline said quickly. "Jacob and I did—"

"I'm well aware of what you and Jacob did," Marion snapped. "You made it perfectly clear when you called me last night what you and Jacob intended to do." Caroline's cheeks turned bright scarlet, but Marion didn't appear to notice. "Which is neither here nor there. We promised this Wyoming fellow—"

"Montana," Dani said wearily.

"—a bride, but I don't remember that we promised him a virgin bride. So we'll write last night off as a premarital fling, and—"

"It was not a premarital fling!" Caroline's cheeks burned. "Or it was, but not in the way you mean! Jacob and I are getting married, and—"

"You're doing no such thing," Marion retorted impatiently. "I'm not having you running off to marry some man I've never met just to spite—"

"I *wanted* you to meet him, but you kept telling me to stop being so silly! You never listen to a word I say, Marion. You didn't even *ask* me before hiring Dani to find me a husband. You didn't even—"

"What the hell," growled a gravelly baritone from the bedroom doorway, "is all the racket about?"

There was a startled gasp from someone, and then—as three sets of eyes swiveled to look at the intruder—absolute silence. Jake glowered sleepily at the three of them, his hair tousled, his cheeks rough with golden-red stubble. He'd pulled his jeans on but hadn't buttoned them, and they gaped, making it fairly obvious he wasn't wearing anything underneath. And he was, Dani decided with an inner glow, the most gorgeous thing she'd ever set eyes on.

"My God," Marion whispered. "He looks like Apollo." Then she wrenched her eyes off Jake with an effort and looked at Dani. "I am so sorry for intruding. It never occurred to me that you might have company—well, I am sorry!"

Caroline nodded miserably. "Me, too."

Dani drew in a deep breath. "Actually, I'm glad you're all here. It's going to save us a lot of time." She took another fortifying breath. "Everybody, I'd like you to meet Jake Montana."

This time the silence was even deeper and longer. Jacob rolled his eyes skyward with a whispered "Oh, boy!" But Caroline and Marion simply stared at Jake, speechless.

Marion recovered first. "Well," she said stiffly, "I knew you took your work seriously, Miss Ross, but I think this is carrying things to extremes. I told you to kick his tires, not take him for a test drive!"

"Look, lady," Jake growled, taking a step forward.

"Jake!" Dani sprang between them, holding her hands out in a conciliatory gesture. "Jake, this is Marion Wainwright-Syms, the woman who—"

"Hired you to find a husband for my sister," Marion said dangerously. "Not to entertain yourself at my expense! What in God's name is going on here?"

"It's . . . well, it's kind of hard to explain, but—"

"It's not hard to explain at all," Jake rasped. "We—"

"Jake, *please*!" Dani shot him a ferocious look, which he ignored.

Then Caroline suddenly stepped forward. She looked up at Jake with an expression of grim determination that closely matched his. "Mr. Montana, I'm Caroline Wainwright, the woman you're going to marry. Or were supposed to marry, that is. Now I'm sure you're a very nice man and I hate to do this with no warning or anything, but I'm sorry, I'm going to marry someone else." She stopped for a breath, and Jake simply stared down at her in bewilderment.

"Jacob and I—That's Jacob over there. He teaches ancient languages at the university. Jacob and I fell in love nearly a year ago, and we're going to get married in spite of what my sister says. I'm terribly sorry to get your hopes up and then dash them like this, but I hope you'll understand. You'll be reimbursed for your plane tickets out here, of course and—"

"I believe he and Miss Ross were about to apologize to *you*, darling," Jacob said quietly, coming over to stand beside her. He looked up at Jake and smiled. "Am I correct, Mr. Montana?"

Jake grinned lazily. "Pretty sharp for a college prof."

"Apologize to me?" Caroline looked from one to the other.

"Caroline," Jake said gently, "I flew out to tell you that I can't marry you."

"You can't?"

"He's marrying Dani," Jacob explained.

"He is?" Caroline blinked owlishly again. Then her face suddenly cleared. "He is! Oh, that's fantastic!" She catapulted herself at Jake, planting an exuberant kiss on his cheek. "Oh, that's marvelous! Isn't that marvelous, Jacob? Dani, you don't know how happy this makes me! I don't mean just because now I don't have to worry about hurting his feelings—I mean I do, but I don't really—but because it's so great for you and—"

"Miss Ross." Marion's voice cut through Caroline's excited chatter. "I did not hire you to find *yourself* a husband."

"It was hardly in my plans, either," Dani said quietly. "I'll see that you're fully reimbursed."

"You most assuredly will. Caroline, stop babbling. You're coming home with me. And you're going to forget all this nonsense about you and Jacob marrying. Jacob, I don't mean to be rude, but you're not what I had in mind when—"

"Marion, I love your sister and I'm going to marry her."

"You most certainly are not going—"

Dani caught Jake's eye across the room and smiled, and Marion's angry voice faded into insignificance. He strolled toward her with that renegade grin, and she felt her heart give a tiny leap of sheer joy. Happily she slipped into his embrace when he reached for her. "Good morning," she whispered.

"Good morning, buttercup." He kissed her lightly.

Behind him, Caroline, her sister and Jacob were standing nose to nose, all of them shouting at once. The din rose, but Dani hardly heard it. "How about some coffee?"

"Tell me you love me first."

"I love you first," she complied promptly. "And fore-most and forever."

"Tell me that you'll marry me."

"I'll marry you." She lifted herself onto her toes to kiss him. "Do you think Cassie would be upset if we had a baby right away?"

"She'd love it," Jake purred. "And so would I. Are you . . . ?"

"I have no idea, although it's certainly possible." Dani smiled. "It's just that I want it all!"

"You've got it, buttercup." He kissed her for a long, sat-isfying while. "Why don't we go back to bed?" he mur-mured. "I doubt this bunch will even notice we're gone."

"A little noisy for sleeping, isn't it?"

"Sleeping wasn't what I had in mind." His smile was warm and private. "Have I told you in the past five min-utes how much I love you, Dani Ross?"

"How much, cowboy?"

"Watch this." He winked at her, then put two fingers in his mouth and gave an ear-shattering whistle that brought an instant and attentive silence. "Folks, it's been real nice meeting you. I know you've all still got a lot to sort out, but I'd appreciate it if you'd do it elsewhere. I want to make love to my wife-to-be and, frankly, you're in the way."

There was an assortment of gasps, none louder than Dani's. Then Jacob chuckled. "Mr. Montana, I admire your style, sir. I hope you'll both come by and have supper with Caroline and me before you head back to B.C."

"That, Jacob, is a promise." Jake shook the proffered hand warmly, then leaned down and kissed Caroline on the cheek. "And if we both hadn't fallen in love and ruined it all, Caroline, I'd have been happy to have married you."

She blushed prettily. Marion snorted and stalked toward the door. "I don't understand any of you," she said crisply, "but I damn well expect invitations to *both* weddings!"

"Both?" Caroline squeaked. "Marion, you mean—?"

"For heaven's sake, Caroline, I run a multimillion dollar corporation. I know when I've been outgunned. Now will you both hurry up! We have to discuss the reception and call the designer for your gown. And these two—" she honored Dani and Jake with a faintly amused look "—have made it abundantly clear that we're not wanted."

She was still machine-gunning orders as the door closed behind them. Dani pressed the backs of her hands to her burning cheeks and laughed. "I can't believe you said that!"

"Now we're even for that bombshell you dropped on *me* with Claudia Schefer," he reminded her with a slashing smile. "Now where were we . . . ?"

*   *   *   *   *

Silhouette Romance®

LONG, TALL TEXANS

AWARD OF EXCELLENCE

Diana Palmer brings you the second Award of Excellence title

SUTTON'S WAY

In Diana Palmer's bestselling Long, Tall Texans trilogy, you had a mesmerizing glimpse of Quinn Sutton—a mean, lean Wyoming wildcat of a man, with a disposition to match.

Now, in September, Quinn's back with a story of his own. Set in the Wyoming wilderness, he learns a few things about women from snowbound beauty Amanda Callaway—and a lot more about love.

He's a Texan at heart . . . who soon has a Wyoming wedding in mind!

The Award of Excellence is given to one specially selected title per month. Spend September discovering *Sutton's Way* #670 . . . only in Silhouette Romance.

READERS' COMMENTS ON
SILHOUETTE INTIMATE MOMENTS:

"About a month ago a friend loaned me my first Silhouette. I was thoroughly surprised as well as totally addicted. Last week I read a Silhouette Intimate Moments and I was even more pleased. They are the best romance series novels I have ever read. They give much more depth to the plot, characters, and the story is fundamentally realistic. They incorporate tasteful sex scenes, which is a must, especially in the 1980's. I only hope you can publish them fast enough."

S.B.*, Lees Summit, MO

"After noticing the attractive covers on the new line of Silhouette Intimate Moments, I decided to read the inside and discovered that this new line was more in the line of books that I like to read. I do want to say I enjoyed the books because they are so realistic and a lot more truthful than so many romance books today."

J.C., Onekama, MI

"I would like to compliment you on your books. I will continue to purchase all of the Silhouette Intimate Moments. They are your best line of books that I have had the pleasure of reading."

S.M., Billings, MT

*names available on request

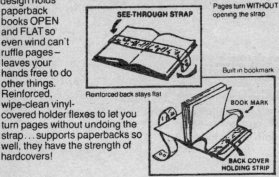

FOUR UNIQUE SERIES
FOR EVERY WOMAN YOU ARE...

Silhouette Romance

Love, at its most tender, provocative, emotional... in stories that will make you laugh and cry while bringing you the magic of falling in love.

6 titles per month

Silhouette Special Edition

Sophisticated, substantial and packed with emotion, these powerful novels of life and love will capture your imagination and steal your heart.

6 titles per month

Silhouette Desire

Open the door to romance and passion. Humorous, emotional, compelling—yet always a believable and sensuous story—Silhouette Desire never fails to deliver on the promise of love.

6 titles per month

Silhouette Intimate Moments

Enter a world of excitement, of romance heightened by suspense, adventure and the passions every woman dreams of. Let us sweep you away.

4 titles per month